Heart of the Bear Champion

ARCTURUS CHAMPIONS
BOOK ONE

OPHELIA BELL

Copyright © 2024 by Ophelia Bell

Cover design by Willsin Rowe

All rights reserved.

No part of this book may be reproduced in any form or by any electronic or mechanical means, including information storage and retrieval systems, without written permission from the author, except for the use of brief quotations in a book review.

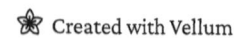

Created with Vellum

FOREWORD

This book was previously published as *The Way to a Bear's Heart* as part of Milly Taiden's Paranormal Dating Agency world, a world which Milly opened up to other authors to write within. It has since been revised to remove mention of Milly's characters and stand on its own as the first book in the "Arcturus Champions" series (formerly "Aurora Champions"). The romance itself remains unchanged from the original. Only certain details that originally drew from Milly's world have been changed. All parts of this story are wholly the creation of Ophelia Bell (and with permission some parts belong to Godiva Glenn, who has several other Celestial Soul Mates books to check out).

CHAPTER
ONE

Liora Delphine settled down at her desk and took a sip of tea. She tapped her mouse to switch her net feed to Arcturus Nebula on one screen while she worked her way through her email on the other. The Arena League season was over, and with its end came the end of an era. The Blackpaw had retired, which meant she expected a call from him any day now, requesting Celestial Soul Mates' services to find him a mate.

She listened to the Arcturus Nebula newsfeed with one ear while she filed messages, always on the lookout for the ones she could act on immediately. News of Blackpaw's retirement had gradually dwindled now that the season was over, making way for buzz about the annual Hot Wings summer bet.

Shaking her head, she tutted softly. Champions were an odd, superstitious bunch who believed mating in their prime was a recipe for failure. True, the Champions with the most successful careers had been unmated. Blackpaw was one example, as was the Ebon Claw, who was still in his prime and going strong. But their beliefs were nothing more than superstition. Someday they'd figure out that having a strong relationship with a mate only made them more invincible.

She'd be ready for them when they figured it out. In the meantime, she would happily make her wager for the annual contest to see which of the Hot Wings duo bedded the most women during their summer off. Her money was going on Bryer Vargas this year.

As Liora glanced away from the newsfeed, one email caught her eye. Ah, there was the one she was looking for. "I'm Ready," was all the subject line said, and the return address was from Astreia, the oldest planet in the Arcturus Nebula. The Blackpaw had emailed her to tell her he'd be on Earth soon and wanted to meet.

"I'm a step ahead of you, Gaius Osborn."

The next email, from a woman who had been a thorn in Liora's side for the past two decades, would hopefully be the answer to Gaius Osborn's request.

"Oh, dear," she said when she read the email from Nina Baxter. She immediately opened her desk drawer and took out her communicator.

She placed the cross-galaxy call, and a second later, a vivid hologram appeared of a solemn-looking woman close to Liora's age. Deep lines of grief framed her eyes.

"Ms. Delphine. Thank you so much for calling."

"Nina, please. We've known each other for more than twenty years. You can call me Liora. I am so sorry to hear the news. How are you and Nessa holding up?"

Nina Baxter's lip quivered and she wrung her hands. "Oh, as well as can be expected. Gordon passed in his sleep. He is at peace now, but I fear Nessa is taking it much harder than I expected."

Liora nodded. "She and her father were always very close."

She avoided venturing into the topic she knew Nina really wanted to discuss. The woman would have to broach it herself if she wanted Liora to take action.

Nina was a sweetheart of a bear shifter, but an opportunist to the core. Liora had always suspected Nina had mated Gordon Baxter for his connections to the upper classes of the shifter community. As a renowned chef, those connections allowed Nina to rub elbows with families such as the Karstens, the rich dragon shifter family her husband had been employed by for much of his career. And more recently, she had begun working her way up the social ranks of the southern Hill Clans, thanks to that recognition.

"Well, Liora, you know how much I love my daughter. I hate to see her hurting. I think the best way to help is to finally find her a mate. Have you had any luck? The clan leaders' sons are all coming of age within the next few years."

"That they are. But it would be unethical of me to orchestrate a date unless they have reached out to a Celestial Soul Mates Oracle asking for one. They may have already reached out to one of my counterparts here on Earth and there would be no way for me to know. I can't interfere with another Oracle's work. Trust that the perfect mate will come along for your daughter when the time is right."

She deliberately remained vague while trying to allay the woman's worries. The inner workings of the Oracles of Celestial Soul Mates was a mystery to the rest of the galaxy, but every Oracle had their own methods and worked in their own unique way. They all drew from the same mystical source, but the truth was a highly guarded secret they would all take to their graves. The important detail was that they were unfailingly accurate at bringing soul mates together among humans and shifters alike.

Nina's brows knit together in a faux frown that Liora saw right through. Now came the manipulating pleas. "Oh, but it must be soon. I'm sure you know how important it is that my daughter mate one of her own kind. She spends so much time with those *dragon boys*. I just can't countenance the idea of her winding up *mated* to one of them."

Liora gritted her teeth in her effort to maintain patience with the other woman. Her husband had just died, so she should tread carefully. The "dragon boys" in question were none other than the Hot Wings duo: Ignazio Karsten and Bryer Vargas. While the pair were most certainly manwhores of the highest degree, they were both honorable men and famous in their own right. Nessa could do a lot worse than having one for a mate.

But Liora had observed them together early on when Nessa's mother had first secured her services as a matchmaker. Nessa had barely been out of diapers at the time, and while Liora preferred to work directly with the individuals who were seeking their own mates, it wasn't unusual for upper-class parents to request the services of an Oracle for their children if a valuable inheritance was on the line. They trusted an Oracle's choices implicitly, and Liora never let them down.

Nina Baxter's intentions were noble, though perhaps a little selfish. Not to mention Nessa Baxter was one of the most headstrong young women Liora had ever met, even as a toddler. She was a lovely, talented young woman now, following in her father's footsteps as a chef, and likely the last thing on her mind would be finding a mate, especially not in the wake of her father's passing. Not all pairings could happen with a single date. Some required more planning, and much more patience.

"I understand your criteria for a mate for Nessa. It's in her file. You need to trust the process, Nina. In fact, I have someone in mind for her who I think is ideal. He's from a noble bear shifter family, and I am meeting with him soon. But even if he *is* ideal, it may not happen right away." She spoke as gently, yet firmly as possible. Parents were the hardest to work with sometimes, and she had to emphasize that finding the perfect mate for someone often wasn't instantaneous.

These two in particular would require some finesse, not to mention placating an anxious, grieving mother who really only wanted to see her daughter happily mated. Both Gaius and Nessa were headstrong, stubborn individuals. The age difference would also likely be a roadblock if she were to attempt to set them up on a blind date.

No . . . their relationship would need to build organically, and if Liora's instincts were correct, Nessa and Gaius were already on a collision course toward each other. With the death of Gordon Baxter, Ignazio Karsten would need a new chef, and Nessa was ideal to fill her father's shoes in that role.

Gaius Osborn was one of Ignazio's oldest friends and had just purchased land near the dragon's northern estate.

If Liora's instincts were right—and they never failed—within the next two years, Nessa and Gaius would be within each other's sights, and from there, fate would take its course.

Nina's lips pinched together as though she were about to protest, but she thought better of it. Good old shifter superstition—Liora's perfect record spoke for itself. Not even Nina's social aspirations would make her question the methods of a matchmaker Oracle.

"Thank you, Liora. Please call me the very second you have a potential mate for Nessa. I hope it's soon."

"You have my word, Nina. Be well."

She ended the call and pulled up her files on the two individuals in question. She'd preemptively created one for Gaius, anticipating his call, and her file for Nessa went back to her mother's first contact around two decades earlier. The Champion had enjoyed a highly successful career in the arena for two full decades, which made him nearly two decades older than Nessa. Bear shifters of the planets in Arcturus Nebula aged slowly, so he was still in his prime, and probably even better mate material for having waited so long.

Nessa she knew less about, but the girl had certainly shown her colors when she was a child, already bossing around her dragon patron's son despite their difference in age. That was one reason she knew for certain Nessa and Ignazio were not mate material for each other. She had the culinary sensibilities to satisfy a dragon, but the wrong temperament to tolerate certain other . . . *appetites* most dragons had.

Gaius was most definitely the man for her. They just needed to receive a little nudge in the right direction.

Liora's meeting with the big Champion the following week only reinforced her conviction that the pair were right for each other. She gave him the same vague directive to "trust the process" and that she would contact him when she found someone. Gaius grumbled a bit, but as an older bear, he would settle into a routine in his retirement. The test would be how he reacted once that routine was disrupted by an enticing, tenacious young woman.

Meanwhile, she fielded monthly calls from Nina Baxter, who was "just checking in" on Liora's progress. Nina received the same reminder that it took time, and Liora made subtle suggestions that Nina give her daughter the freedom to move forward with her career, telling her it was what her late husband would have wanted.

Indeed, it ultimately took nearly two years before the wheels began turning at a quicker pace. It began when Nina called to agonize over her daughter's decision to move to the Karstens' northern estate and fill her role as chef there. Ignazio Karsten was maturing, if he was finally choosing a permanent residence. But it also put Nessa Baxter within a few miles of Gaius, who now had a successful career as a builder.

Everything was falling into place. All Liora needed to do now was watch and wait.

CHAPTER TWO

NESSA

Nessa swallowed her tears. The emotions tangled in her belly were half frustration, half anticipated homesickness. She was eager to get on her way, yet sad to go, and her mother's nervous hovering wasn't helping things.

"I've got to get packed, Mama. Ig's waiting." She surveyed her bedroom for any last-minute items she thought she'd need over the next few months.

"I know, honey. But you know it won't be that long a trip. Oracle Delphine could call any day to tell us she found you a mate. The clan leaders' sons are all at the age when they should find mates, and no doubt they'll be going to her. She's the best matchmaker there is!"

Nessa suppressed a long-suffering sigh and instead just nodded at her mother. "Well, if that happens, I'll be on the next transport home. I promise."

The truth was she put little stock in the likelihood of the matchmaker hooking her up with an actual clan leader's son. That was her mother's dream, not hers. Not that she wouldn't entertain the idea if it happened—the trio of ancient bear shifters who led the Hill Clans all had sons worthy of any woman's attention. But the three elders who made up the council were still hale, robust leaders, and their sons weren't actually required to mate until they assumed the mantles of leadership.

At this stage, it was all just a little girl's fantasy to be the mate of one of them. She'd outgrown those dreams in her father's kitchen, learning to love cooking for their rich dragon patrons. The Karstens felt more like family than any of the southern bear clans did, even though her parents were their employees. She'd grown up with Ignazio, looking up to the young dragon shifter like she would an older brother.

Now that Ignazio was a famous Arena League Champion, he had begun carving his own path. He'd stepped out from his late father's shadow, but hadn't forgotten Nessa's family.

She snapped her luggage closed and turned to give her mother a hug. Her mother's sweet honeysuckle scent pervaded her senses, and she inhaled despite the surge of sadness that nearly overwhelmed her. She wished her father were here to say farewell to her, and to beam and chuff about how proud he was.

"I only want you to be happy, honey, you know that," her mother said softly. "I want you to have what your father and I couldn't give you."

"I know, Mama," Nessa said, wiping her eyes. "But this is what I want more than anything. Now that Papa's gone, it only makes sense for me to work for Ig. And with him moving, it's my chance to . . ." She shrugged. "Have my own kitchen."

She was also ready to step out from her father's shadow, which had lingered long after his death two years earlier. Her dad had been a master chef for more than a century to the Karstens and their entire extended family of dragon shifters. It wasn't as prestigious a position as working for the leader of the Astreia dragon clans, but it was close.

Her mother patted her cheek and gave her a patient smile. "Soon enough you'll have your own staff to cook *for* you. Wouldn't that be wonderful?"

Nessa almost strained herself to avoid rolling her eyes. There was no getting through to her mother that the thing she loved most *was* cooking. It was the closest thing to making magic that she could think of. But then her mother wasn't a chef. It was her father's first love, and he was the one who had instilled that love in Nessa practically since birth.

She hauled her heavy suitcase off the bed and carried it through the door, heading down the stairs with her mother close behind. Ignazio sat at the breakfast table, silently sipping his tea. He looked up when she came in and she gave him a little wave. "Ready when you are."

"Excellent!" he said, standing and approaching her. "Thank you for agreeing to this, Ness. Your dad's old kitchen misses you. You're going to love it at the lake. It'll be like old times."

"Until you're mated, anyway," her mother interjected. "I will call you as soon as I hear from the Oracle."

"Can't wait, Mom!" Nessa gritted through her teeth. She shared another teary hug with her mom, then extracted herself and shut the front door behind her.

"You're not going to run off and get mated on me, are you?" Ignazio asked on the way to his transport. The cargo hold at the back was filled with her belongings. Her kitchen supplies filled one side of the narrow aisle, while the other side was filled with any other things she couldn't live without. He carefully loaded her suitcase in the last available spot before helping her climb up. The loading ramp automatically rose to close them in as they settled in their seats up front.

"Hell no. Mama means well. I think she's always idolized the upper class and sees me as her chance to become part of it before she gets too old to enjoy it."

Ignazio frowned as he started up the transport and they lifted off the ground, hovering in mid-air for a moment while the engines warmed up. "I thought you guys were always happy working for us," he said. "If you ever need anything..."

"Oh! Ig, please. Don't let my mom's behavior give you the wrong idea. I'm beyond thrilled that you asked me to be your chef. And by the way, thank you for not letting it slip that you're renovating the lake house. If Mom knew, she'd have tried to make me wait until it was finished."

"Well, you can't very well give your input on the new kitchen if you aren't there. I've hired one of the best builders for this project. He's ready and waiting to work with you on every detail. And I mean that—whatever you want, you just tell him. You've got carte blanche on the kitchen."

She grinned at him. "I can't wait!"

CHAPTER
THREE
NESSA

"Wow, you're really gutting the place, aren't you?" Nessa said as Ignazio gave her a tour of his lake house and a rundown of his plans for it.

"You have to admit it's pretty dated. But the best part about it was always the view and that's not changing." They paused in the empty interior, gazing out the floor-to-ceiling windows to the lake beyond.

Nessa let out a long sigh. "You got that right. I always loved spending summers here. I don't know why, but these mountains feel more like home than the hills to the south. Now lead on and tell me more about your plans."

They made their way through the house, which was little more than a construction zone. It was quiet at the moment, but smelled like sawdust and plaster.

"Work crews are due to start on the living area tomorrow," Ignazio said. "Gaius should be meeting us here a little later to take a look at the kitchen with you."

"Gaius. He's the master builder you hired to do the kitchen?"

"Well, the whole house, but kitchens are his specialty,

so he's seeing to that part personally. It's *your* kitchen, Nessa. I meant it when I said you can have it any way you want it. You're the best, so you should have the best."

Her kitchen. Nessa chewed on her lip, barely containing the excitement. But when they headed down to the ground floor and through the doors to the room she remembered most fondly, something bothered her.

It was still the same well-worn kitchen. The ancient stove and ovens carried the patina of age and many meals filled with love. She'd acquired her love of the alchemy of flavors here. Mixing spices in the best savory combinations and crafting sweets that were sure to earn the Karstens' praises. But it was darker than she remembered, and smaller somehow. After seeing Ignazio's plans for the rest of the house, this little space didn't fit.

"What is it?" he asked.

"How much flexibility do you have on the plan?"

"A little . . ." he said cautiously.

"Humor me for a few," she said. "Come on."

Nessa led him back out the door, past the training gym that was arguably the closest room to being finished in the entire house, and up the stairs to the back of the house. The rear gardens stretched the entire length of the back of the big house, with the small cottage at one end where she and her parents had spent summers when she was growing up. Her dad had kept a small herb garden near the cottage, while the rest of the gardens were populated by colorful and mostly ornamental foliage.

She stopped in the middle of the garden and smiled at Ignazio's perplexed look.

"You said I had carte blanche, right?"

"Yeah . . ." he said with a cautious drawl. "What are you thinking?"

She took a deep breath and was about to explain her wishes for the kitchen and the garden when a burst of raucous laughter echoed through the rear of the house.

Ignazio's head jerked around and he looked back at her, holding up a hand. "Hold that thought."

Nessa huffed and pressed her lips together. She followed Ignazio to the stretch of glass-paneled doors that lined the rear of the house and what had once been a formal dining room. A pair of shadowy figures were inside, engaged in animated conversation, their deep voices echoing through the empty interior of the house.

Her eyes lit up when she recognized one of the men, and she bounced on her heels in excitement.

"Bryer Vargas, is that you?" she called as Ignazio's Arena partner stepped through the door.

His blue eyes lit up as she bounded into his embrace. "Hey, sexy lady," he said, laughing into her hair and holding her tight.

She slid back to the ground, holding Bryer at arm's length and looking him over with a serious expression. After a second, she nodded. "Yep, you are *definitely* in need of some good home-cooking. What've you been living on lately? Bread and water?"

"You got me, Nessa. I just have no appetite for anything but your delicious treats." His grin turned distinctly wicked as his gaze traveled down her ample curves.

Nessa rolled her eyes. "Oh, stop it. You know I'm not going to fall for your charms, Bry. I'd just wind up a notch in your bedpost for your stupid bet. Besides, you know once you had a taste, you'd be as addicted as you are to my cooking, and far be it from me to deprive all your fans of your sexy behind."

Ignazio let out a bark of laughter. "He also knows I'd

kick his ass if he touched you. Seriously, dude, she *just* got here."

Bryer held up his hands. "I surrender. Just glad you're here, sweet Nessa." He rubbed his hands together greedily. "So, when's dinner?"

"No food until *after* we hear her plans for the kitchen. You guys have perfect timing, though. Nessa, this is Gaius Osborn, the builder I was telling you about. He's an old friend."

The big man standing at Bryer's side seemed to fill her entire field of vision then. For a moment, Nessa was sure time had stopped, and it left her feeling off balance. He had a mop of wild, thick dark hair shot through with silver, and blue eyes nearly as vibrant as Bryer's. His cheeks and chin were covered in a close-cut beard that framed full lips and was similarly peppered with silver strands.

And he was huge. Easily the biggest bear shifter she'd ever seen, he towered over both her friends, who weren't small men by any means.

He looked wary as he held out his hand for her to shake. "You must be this master chef Ig's been goin' on about. So, let's hear your crazy plan."

She took his hand, which engulfed hers in warmth that was at odds with the cool stare he gave her. Confused by the contradictory messages, she shrugged and shook her head, trying to clear it of that odd sensation that had come over her a moment earlier.

"I don't think it's crazy at all," she said. "The garden is where I want to start, actually. The ornamentals are pretty, but a bit of a waste. I want to fill this entire space with culinary plants. Herbs, flowers, fruit trees, everything. It'll be functional *and* ornamental by the time I'm done with it." She spun around once in the garden to take it in, and then darted a look up at Gaius. His gaze snapped away abruptly and his scowl deepened.

"Sounds lovely," Ignazio said. "I have a landscape designer available to do whatever you wish."

"If it's all right, I'd like to do a lot of it myself. I've kind of always loved this part of the property. It means a lot to me to have a hand in the actual work. Adds to the alchemy of the dishes if I grow the ingredients myself."

"Fair enough. You're the boss," Ignazio said. "And the kitchen? Shall we head down there next?"

She stopped in front of the row of doors and turned to face the trio. Gaius tensed. What the hell was up with the guy? She'd have thought he expected her to fire him and declare she wanted to do *that* job herself too.

"Actually, we're there," she said.

Ignazio and Bryer both lifted their eyebrows, as though waiting for the punch line. Gaius' eyes widened for a split second before his lips tightened and tilted into a distinct frown.

"Ah . . . where, exactly?" Ig asked.

"The kitchen! It should be the heart of the home, and that—" she pointed into the house just past the doors "—is right in there. You have to admit the formal dinners your parents threw were always boring as all get out. I think you should repurpose this part of the house. Move the kitchen here, next to the garden. Keep a less formal dining room in the center of the house with a view of the lake."

She paused and absorbed the variety of expressions on the three men. Ignazio rubbed his chin thoughtfully and nodded. Bryer licked his lips, clearly thinking about his next meal—the man was as transparent as they came.

Gaius, however, looked like he was having trouble

holding something in. He practically glared at her, hard enough her hackles rose.

"What?" she asked, facing him and putting her hands on her hips. "Do you have a better plan, Mr. Superstar Builder?"

Gaius grunted and crossed his arms. "Move the kitchen up here, huh? Do you have any idea what kind of impact that'll have on the design for the rest of the house? Plumbing'll have to be rerouted, electrical reconfigured, not to mention the rearranging of the existing layout. Could have a domino effect on the whole damn thing. Don't even want to get into the delays that could cause."

Ignazio clapped him on the shoulder. "I'm sure you're up to it, old buddy. Whatever Nessa wants for this kitchen, she gets. Trust me, she's worth it. Now, I will leave you two to go over the details. Bry and I need to discuss the new rehab center we want to put in down by the training gym now that that space is opening up."

With that, the pair were off, leaving Nessa and Gaius staring each other down.

She refused to be intimidated by the big guy. This was her *dream* at stake, and Ignazio had been gracious enough to allow her the freedom to do it right. There was no way in hell she'd let one big, surly shifter ruin it for her.

"You look like a bear who takes eating seriously," she said after taking his measure. He wasn't fat by any means, but a bear as big as he was didn't stay as fit and deliciously ripped without a generous diet.

Again with the grunting as he stared her down. "What of it?"

"I just think you should appreciate the value a good kitchen design has on the creation of a meal. I'm cooking for dragons. A flexible workspace is going to be necessary."

"Never said I didn't know what goes into a proper kitchen," he said, still stoically regarding her.

Exasperated, she turned on her heel and walked toward the doors. "Well, at least humor me and let me tell you my ideas. Feel free to shoot them down. You *are* the best . . . allegedly." She muttered the last word under her breath as she walked into the bare, sunlit space.

One of the reasons she loved this space was the morning sun that shone in through the wall of glass doors. The wood-framed panes cast crisscrossing shadows along the floor, creating a grid that made it even easier for her to demonstrate her vision.

Halfway through explaining the arrangement of stove, countertops, and pantry, she glanced up to see Gaius staring off into space beyond the doors.

"Are you listening to me? This is where the pantry needs to go. And the cooler will be accessible from inside."

"I hear ya," Gaius said without looking at her. "But that old stove downstairs is going to look mighty out of place in the layout you want, all stainless steel and white tile."

She stared at him, her mouth hanging open for a moment. The old stove. Her father's old kitchen. Hesitantly, she shook her head. "It'll work." Darting her gaze around the space, she tried to rearrange her plan in her mind to make room for the old equipment she loved so much.

Without looking back, she turned and headed out into the vast, empty house and down the back stairs to the old kitchen. Her gut churned with uncertainty. She'd been so gung-ho about her new dream kitchen that she'd forgotten to make room in it for the old one.

She pushed through the swinging doors into the old space, and the comforting scents washed over her anew. All her father's favorite spices brought back memories of helping him prepare meals for the Karstens over the years. But Gaius was right; none of the pieces of equipment in here fit her vision of the new kitchen. She'd spent many sleepless nights since Ignazio's suggestion that she take her father's place looking at catalogs of kitchen equipment. She had her heart set on new, top-of-the-line pieces, and couldn't get the image out of her head of the finished kitchen, all gleaming stainless steel and white tile lit up by the morning sun as she started her day.

Her father's stove, with its worn enamel, copper accents, and ancient gauges and knobs, belonged in another era, even if it was still fully functional.

She sensed the big bear come through the doors and stop. He stood quietly, looking around with a serene expression. When he met her gaze, his brows lifted. "It's not the end of the world," he said. "You still gotta cook while I'm fitting out the new kitchen anyway, right? Though it'll be a shame to see this torn down at the end."

He wandered to the far end of the kitchen and hit a worn button on the wall, summoning the clanking old dumbwaiter that had delivered the meals to the floor above. He grunted in amusement as the doors opened. "Don't make 'em like they used to," he said softly.

Having lost her enthusiasm for the planning, she sat on a stool and sighed. "I grew up in this kitchen, you know."

Gaius came around the big chopping block island and rapped his knuckles on it, then bent down and eyed the surface appreciatively. He made a gruff sound of interest and looked up at her.

"I learned to cook here," she continued. "And in the kitchen at the Karstens' estate in the south. But this was always my favorite place. They had the best parties during the summer seasons here."

"Off-season," Gaius said, nodding. "Well, for Champions, at least. Karstens always did know how to throw a party."

"Were you a fan?" Nessa asked, remembering that Ignazio had introduced Gaius as an old friend.

His brows twitched. "You could say that." Standing up, he added, "Well, I think I've got enough to get started. You enjoy the memories. This place is sure thick with them."

Before she could respond, he'd turned and walked back through the doors, his shoulders practically brushing both sides of the doorjamb.

Nessa sat in the silence for several minutes, simply absorbing the atmosphere and letting all those old memories wash over her. New was good . . . she knew that. If she was going to start her own life, she needed to do it on her terms. As much as she had learned working beside her father, she had no intention of becoming his clone. She had her own recipes along with old favorites, and had always loved adding her own twist to things. This was no different.

With a sigh, she slid off the stool and shifted gears. She still had work to do. Ignazio hadn't hired her to sit on her butt and feel maudlin all day. After she finished their midday meal, she'd go up and start mapping out a plan for the garden.

CHAPTER
FOUR
GAIUS

Gaius winced at the pain in his knees, the old arena combat injury warning that hot, humid weather was coming. Funny thing was he'd felt no pain for the last hour while Nessa was going on about her kitchen. All he'd felt then was irritation at having a spitfire of a young woman telling *him* how to build a damn kitchen.

She'd had such dreamy light in her eyes as she bounced through the big, empty space. She practically danced from imaginary stove to imaginary counter, waving her graceful hands and describing the whole place in such vivid detail he could easily picture it himself.

That annoyed him too. She couldn't have known he already intended to suggest Ig move the kitchen and was dreading the wrangling he'd have to do to get the stubborn dragon shifter to see reason. Yet there waltzed in this pretty little bear who clearly had both the Hot Wings boys wrapped around her little finger, and all she had to do was smile that sweet, dimply smile and Ig caved.

He snorted as he pulled out the plans and unfurled them across a makeshift table he'd set up in the center of the empty space that'd soon be Nessa's dream kitchen. She had a good sense of space, that was for sure. Everything she'd described had been more or less how he'd imagined the place looking, only nicer, he had to admit. Pity that her old man's kitchen wouldn't fit. He already knew once the new kitchen was built, the old one would likely wind up recycled for raw materials. Ig wanted a new rehab center down there and the old kitchen's location was ideal.

He eyeballed the updated plans, making little tweaks here and there. It was far less complicated than he'd let on, and the plans for the rest of the house somehow flowed effortlessly out of that central hub.

His nose twitched and his stomach rumbled. Some delicious aroma had started to fill the room, and he lifted his head to stare at the old dumbwaiter on the far wall where the scent was emanating from.

With a growl of frustration, he packed up the plans and left. It was tricky enough having her on his mind when he was working; the distraction of her cooking would do him no good. He wasn't due to start work until the next day and could make the rest of his calls from home.

Home. Such as it was.

He parked his little solo transport in the gravel driveway and stared up at the skeleton framework of the house he'd started almost a year ago and had yet to finish. The empty window frames stared back accusingly and he grumbled as he stalked past to the outdoor kitchen he'd constructed on his deck. The outer deck and frame of the house was more or less complete, but the interior was something he had lacked the necessary motivation to finish.

Once he'd thrown together a cold lunch, he grabbed his communicator and stared at it while he chewed. He scrolled down, searching for the number of the building supplier. The Oracle's name popped up on the little screen and his finger itched to call. It wasn't because he was desperate. He'd only been retired from the Arena League for two seasons. After decades of single life, he was in no hurry to settle down. Being a bachelor suited him just fine.

Yet he'd given Liora Dephine his info the very day of his retirement, then bought this land and started constructing this house the following week. The house that he intended for his eventual mate.

He growled and tossed his communicator aside. She'd call when she found someone. *If* she found someone.

Resolving to make his calls before dinner, Gaius dug into his meal, enjoying the cold spiced meat sandwich and the spectacular midday view—his own little piece of paradise in the mountains of Astreia.

But for some reason that afternoon, the usually comforting solitude felt more like exile. After a leisurely shower under the nearby waterfall followed by a long soak in his swimming hole, he still couldn't shake the sense of loneliness.

Later, as he climbed into the hammock strung between two posts on his front porch where he could see the stars, he couldn't stop picturing Nessa's troubled frown as she stared wistfully around the old kitchen. And instead of falling asleep to the sight of moonrise, he drifted off with the first image he'd had of her that day, spinning around in the garden among the flowers like some fertility goddess.

CHAPTER
FIVE
NESSA

The next morning, Nessa served breakfast in the same spot where the prior two meals had been served: on the outdoor dining table that had been moved down from the deck to the patio outside Ignazio's training gym. It made sense in the interim to have meals served there, since the house was a disaster area and its owner spent the majority of his time in his gym during the off-season, anyway.

Bryer was in attendance again, looking chipper, though not exactly well-rested. Nessa recognized the satisfied exhaustion following a night well spent in some groupie's bed and chuckled to herself.

After setting out the main dishes, she went back to the kitchen for some extra servings of protein. Both men were in rare form this summer, already well on their way to wearing out the single women of the region on their annual off-season bet. She imagined said women were not complaining, though.

"Come sit with us!" Bryer called.

"No thanks, honey. You both still smell like sex. Do me a favor and shower before lunch?"

"I do not..." Bryer said, dipping his head to take a whiff of himself. Then he leaned over and inhaled close to Ignazio's shoulder. "Hmm, foxy. Did we both wind up with the same girl last night?"

Ignazio shook his head. "Twins," he muttered around a mouthful of food.

Nessa just shook her head indulgently and headed up the outdoor steps to the rear of the house, ready to work on the garden for a little while before lunch. Her stomach knotted when she saw the doors to the interior propped open and heard the sounds of power tools coming from within. As she drew close, the warm scent of cut wood hit her nostrils. She had walked through the empty space on her way down to the kitchen at dawn that morning, and it'd been peaceful and dead quiet.

But now the place was completely different, with the beginnings of cabinets and countertops lining the walls and the floors marked with crisscrossing lines of red and blue chalk marking out the areas where she'd described wanting the different pieces to go.

She wandered through while Gaius was busy cutting and stopped at one conspicuously empty section by the wall with a heavy, rough board nailed over it. It looked messy and unprofessional, to say the least, unlike the rest of the neatly arranged beginnings of the buildout.

"What the hell?" she muttered, then turned to look at Gaius. He turned off the saw and hoisted a big length of wood up over one shoulder, carrying it toward the far wall where he held it in place at about hip-height. He apparently hadn't seen or heard her, so she waited in irritation, torn between griping at him about the messy wall treatment and not interrupting what looked to be a rather intricate construction he was working on. His big biceps bunched under the strain of holding up the piece of wood as he carefully fitted each end into notches she realized were already in place in the existing frame. Maybe they were meant to be cabinets at some point.

Nessa cleared her throat. "I've got a question!" she called to his back.

Gaius tensed, but didn't turn. He only twitched a shoulder and bent to start hammering at the wood in front of him. Nessa tilted her head, distracted by the ripple of the muscles beneath his shirt and the way his big thigh flexed as he half-knelt over where the wood was joined. After a moment, he stopped and turned, only giving her a cursory glance before his gaze darted to the wall that she was emphatically pointing at.

"What's this?"

"Old dumbwaiter. That's just temporary until I can rip the damn thing out. Figured I wouldn't interrupt your cooking to do it. I'll get it first thing tomorrow, if that's all right with you. Unless you intended to deliver me food while I work."

"Oh. I guess . . ." she said, feeling about as dumb as the dumbwaiter.

"Forget it. Ig didn't hire you to feed me." He gave her a sardonic look before turning back to the saw to begin cutting another piece.

"So, it's looking . . ." She tried to find something nice to say, but the place wasn't much to look at despite the obvious signs he'd made significant progress that morning.

Gaius cut her off. "If you don't mind, I've got countertops scheduled to be delivered in the morning. Want to get these lower cabinets installed today. Unless you have any changes?"

He crossed his arms and glared at her as though daring her to mess with his plans again. All Nessa could see was how huge his chest and arms looked whenever he stood that way.

She let out a little huff and shook her head, mostly to clear it of the strange warmth that had risen up from deep inside. "Not at all. You just go on about your cabinetmaking. I'm going to work out in the garden for a few. If you want my input on anything, you know where to find me."

"That I do," he said, sounding for all the world like he had zero intention of asking for her input if he could help it.

Nessa stalked through the door, strangely irked by his dismissal. She headed to the cottage at the far end of the garden, where she changed into shorts and a loose-fitting halter top that both supported her generous bosom and let her skin breathe in the heat. She re-pinned her hair more securely and grabbed her work gloves, then stalked back into the garden, ready to rip out some useless vines while imagining ripping the surly carpenter a new one.

She'd just started tearing at the foliage along the back wall when she heard a voice calling her name. Preparing to launch her mentally rehearsed tirade at the big bear, she turned and had to bite her tongue.

"Man, aren't you a sight for sore eyes!" A tall, lanky shifter Nessa hadn't seen in years loped over to her and lifted her in a welcome hug.

"Levi! Wow! You got . . . big," she said, laughing when he released her. The young cheetah shifter had been barely more than a cub the last time she'd seen him. She stood back to take him in and shook her head. "Already a ladykiller, look at you! What are you doing here?"

"I work here now. Ig and Bry hired me as their assistant. That means doing whatever you need me to do today, according to Ig." He stuck his thumbs in his pockets and surveyed her destruction with a frown. "So, angry weeding, is it?"

Nessa snorted. "Not angry, just enthusiastic. I want to turn this section into the nightshade vines. They'll flower nice in springtime and be filled with fruit in the summer and fall. Figured I'd work my way in from the garden walls. The paths will be lined with Astreian Dewpetal flowers, and I'll put raised herb beds outside the kitchen doors with benches along one side."

Levi listened, enraptured, and followed her around the garden while she gave him a tour, all the while describing her plans for the various fruit trees and vegetable patches she planned. In her mind, the garden was already a magical labyrinth of culinary wonders, and all hers. She even managed to mostly forget about the arousing sight of the big bear who was still hammering away inside her kitchen.

CHAPTER
SIX
GAIUS

Gaius lost track of his senses when the curvy young woman came back out of her little cottage wearing half the amount of clothing she'd worn moments ago. He'd been standing at his saw and glanced up in time for her to bend over and start yanking at some offending plant or other. The sight of her ripe, round backside wiggling to and fro made his mouth go dry and his cock stand stiff inside his jeans. He barely had the presence of mind to turn off the power to the saw before losing a finger.

Cursing under his breath, he turned and set the next crosspiece in place, hammering harder than necessary to get it seated. All he could think about was her adorably irritated face when she thought he'd ruined her kitchen with the stupid board over the dumbwaiter. It seemed like she got more beautiful the more emotional she was, and that gorgeous, round ass of hers was stirring some pretty intense feelings in him too.

He scraped his fingernails up and down the back of his head and shook it, trying to dispel that vision. But he couldn't help it. He had to look again, just to see if she was real, even if she drove him mad with her ability to read his mind.

But when he glanced out the door again, his blood ran hot. Some unfamiliar male had his goddamned arms around her.

"Oh, hell no," he growled and started for the door. He was about to step out and pummel the interloper when logic kicked in. "She is not your fucking mate, dude," he whispered to himself. "Get a grip."

She was probably the *last* woman he needed for a mate. As bossy as she was, they'd tear each other to pieces if left alone together for five minutes, he was sure of it. Yet he kept watching from the shadows while she gave the guy a tour, chattering animatedly the entire time. The man eventually produced a pair of work gloves and settled in beside her, tearing out vines and happily complying with her every direction.

Eventually, the uncomfortable sense of intrusion subsided. She'd been no more than casually friendly to the guy and was clearly comfortable bossing him around. Oddly, that didn't make Gaius feel any better. Was she bossy like that to *every* man she knew?

He went back to his work with a strange, tightness in his chest. For the next few hours, he went about the project on autopilot, unable to shake the overwhelming need to walk out into the garden and stake his claim on her.

He was busy framing out the corner where the new pantry would go when someone rapped on the door behind him. His heart lurched and his cock twitched in his pants at the possibility of her presence, but the scent that reached him a second later was distinctly not hers. *Male cat* was his impression, and he let out an involuntary growl as he turned.

"Whoa," said the tall, scruffy shifter who'd had his arms around Nessa. "Ig didn't warn me you were so territorial. I just wanted to see if you needed anything. I'm Levi . . . Ig and Bry's assistant."

Gaius half-raised the hammer in his fist. Levi eyed the tool with a worried frown.

"And what're you to her?" Gaius asked, not even sure where the question came from.

Levi's eyes widened. He glanced out the window where Nessa was standing with the garden hose raised over her head, her face tilted to the sky as the water cascaded into her mouth and over her sweet curves. She was turned away, and what Gaius wouldn't give to see the front of her top all soaked through.

"Nessa's an old friend. That's all. Like . . . like a big sister. Seriously, you don't have to worry about me. I didn't even know she had a mate."

The statement hit Gaius like a cold slap. "I'm not her mate," he snapped.

Levi tilted his head. "Whatever you say, man. I just came in to check whether you need anything. I can help with the labor, make calls, anything."

Gaius eyed him warily, gradually realizing he must look like a fucking crazy person holding his hammer up like he was ready to pummel the guy with it. He forced himself to relax.

"You should keep helping her," he muttered.

"Well, I plan to again tomorrow. She's stopping for the day, though. It's too damn hot out there, for one thing, and she's got to go get lunch started for the guys."

Gaius nodded and glanced back out the window. Nessa had the hose aimed straight up her shirt now and was angled slightly toward the window, apparently oblivious that there might be observers on the other side of the glass.

He cleared his throat and shook his head to clear it of her perfect profile, dripping wet and more luscious than he could stand. "Ah, do you mind asking her if I can tear out the dumbwaiter this afternoon? I know it's a bit soon..."

"Sure thing!" Levi darted back out the door quicker than Gaius could track. Nessa jumped when Levi said her name, and turned to fully face the bank of windows.

Gaius' pulse quickened. Her top was snug around her big, perfect breasts, a layer of its fabric flowing over her belly, and it was soaked through so thoroughly that she may as well have been dressed in tissue paper. Her brown nipples were visible through the waterlogged fabric, and the rest of it clung to her abdomen darkly, aside from a lighter section where it spanned the indentation of her navel.

Water dripped off her chin and she turned her gaze to the interior, blinking wet lashes. For a moment, Gaius froze, sure he'd been caught staring, but she didn't seem to register his presence. Regardless, he forced himself to turn around, deciding to preemptively yank the cover off the dumbwaiter hoping she'd say yes.

He'd pried the wood off and tossed it aside when Levi's footsteps returned. "She asked if you wouldn't mind waiting. If it's going to cause a mess, she'd rather you do it when she's not about to go down to cook, and man, you really don't want to interfere with her cooking... have you tasted the things she can make?"

"Haven't had the pleasure," Gaius said, forcing his disappointment aside. Working on removing this thing would require him to spend time in the old kitchen, and for some reason, he had the strongest urge to be closer to her.

"Ah, that is just too bad. Maybe if you're sweet to her, she'll give you a taste sometime. It's worth it."

Levi had delivered the remark with complete innocence, but it still made Gaius heat again with territorial rage.

Levi's eyes widened for the second time. "Chill out, bro! I didn't mean it *that* way."

"Are you sure?" Gaius sneered. "How can you not see how perfect she is? She was on full display to you just now. Don't tell me that didn't affect you." He stabbed his finger at the window, but Nessa had disappeared.

Levi's throat rippled with a nervous swallow. "Ah . . . you mean with the water? I've known Nessa since I was a kid. We played naked together. Shifting and swimming in the lake . . . Don't hit me! I mean, I appreciate how gorgeous she is, but I really have zero interest in her that way! I've always believed I'd know my mate when I saw her. When I look at Nessa, it's just . . . " He shrugged. "Friendly. I love her, but not that way."

"Like a sister," Giaus said, relaxing for the first time in a while.

"Yeah, and for the record, I guarantee that's how Ig and Bry feel too."

With a frustrated chuff, Gaius sagged back against the half-built cabinetry behind him. He raked his hands through his hair and shook his head. "What the fuck is wrong with me?"

Levi took a cautious step closer. "Seems like you like her more. A lot more. Is that a bad thing?"

"I just fucking met her and she's . . ."

"Under your skin?" Levi offered.

"Driving me batshit with her . . . bossiness."

Levi laughed. "Yeah, that's Nessa. She's always known

what she wants and doesn't hesitate to tell whoever will listen. It grows on you, trust me."

"Don't know if I can deal," Gaius said, giving the kid a helpless look.

Levi regarded him solemnly. "Well, if you don't want to wind up in love with her, I don't recommend tasting her food. Me and Ig and Bry are all half in love just from that. You can bet if we believed she was our mate, the claws would come out."

Gaius chuckled ruefully. "I don't get the sense she likes me much. I think I'll just keep my head down and focus on the project, if it's all the same to you."

"Fair enough," Levi said. "Anything else I can do for you? Nessa related or not..."

"Actually you could make some calls, if you don't mind. It'd save me a hassle later if all I have to worry about is the construction here. And later this week, I'm laying tile. If you're up for manual labor, I could use a hand. It'll save my old knees the strain."

Levi eagerly agreed and whipped a small tablet out of his pocket to take down the instructions. The kid was quick; Gaius had to give him that. Even if his gut still churned over his unexpected reaction to Nessa, some of his tension eased to have an assistant handle the calls he needed to make, and some of the grunt work that no longer agreed with his old injuries. According to the weather report, the pain in his knees was only going to get worse as the week went on.

Levi was about to leave when Gaius called out, "Hey, kid. One more thing."

Levi looked at him with such openness Gaius wondered how he'd ever felt threatened by him. "Whatever you need!"

"Do me a favor and don't tell Ig or Bry about . . . this. They'd never let me hear the end of it."

Levi laughed. "Secret's safe with me. Just be careful. She's important to us."

"Who's important to you?" a chirpy voice said from the door. Gaius tensed like he'd been electrocuted, and it took an effort of will to force himself to relax when Nessa sauntered through his workspace and paused at the door beside Levi.

"Why, you are, of course," Levi said, nonchalantly. "Why else would Ig let you torture one of his best friends so you could have the kitchen of your dreams?"

"Oh, come on," Nessa said, smacking Levi on the arm and rolling her eyes at Gaius. "They just love me for my sticky buns."

Gaius snorted and shook his head, resolving to refocus for the rest of the afternoon so he didn't get too far behind schedule. She'd already distracted him enough for one day.

The lanky shifter loped off, but Nessa remained behind, watching him. His skin prickled under her scrutiny.

He glanced at her with a soft grunt of inquiry.

"Tortured, huh?" She crossed her arms, obscuring his view of the most delicious pair of breasts he'd seen in ages. "I mean, if you're really that eager to get rid of the stupid dumbwaiter, I can try to work around the interference."

The bite to her voice told Gaius she was less than eager to accommodate him. That stung worse than it should have.

"Don't do me any damn favors. I promise it'll be taken care of when I can get to it and it won't interfere with your precious cooking."

"Fine. You don't have to be so damn pissy about it." She stalked off in a huff, and Gaius was glad he hadn't framed out the wall and installed the door yet. She'd have probably slammed it if he had.

About half an hour later, the most delicious scents wafted up, courtesy of the dumbwaiter shaft. An hour after that, when his stomach was growling louder than his angry Uncle Buster on a bender, a clank echoed up the shaft, followed by a grinding sound as the dumbwaiter's motor kicked into gear. He stared at it like it was some alien beast preparing to attack.

The small car screeched to a stop, the scent of some savory, freshly baked treat betraying the nature of whatever lurked on the other side of the rolling door.

Gaius' mouth watered and his stomach rumbled so loud it echoed. He'd packed a lunch, but there was no way in hell what he'd made for himself would be as good as whatever she'd just sent up.

He took a cautious step toward the dumbwaiter and reached out. Grabbing the handle with thumb and forefinger, he peeked underneath. A slip of paper came into view that said, "Peace offering."

He lifted the door farther to display the big plateful of food and licked his lips. Big, thickly cut fried potatoes were piled on one side of the plate, and on the other was the biggest, juiciest burger, piled with toppings and cheese. She couldn't have known . . . No way in hell could she have known he'd spent six months on Earth after his semi-enforced retirement from the League. While he was there, he'd tried just about every food humanity had to offer, and the one thing he knew he'd always remember fondest was the cheeseburger.

"If you don't want to wind up in love with her, I don't recommend tasting her food."

Gaius stared at the meal like it was about to leap off the

plate. He snatched the piece of paper and flipped it over, scrawled a quick note on it, then shoved it back under the plate and slammed the dumbwaiter door shut. Only when the thing was headed back south did he finally let out a long breath.

Feeling like he'd just dodged a bullet, he immediately went to the corner where his lunch was stashed and carried it out into the garden to eat. If there's one thing he'd learned, it was not to deal with bossy women on an empty stomach.

CHAPTER
SEVEN
NESSA

Nessa stared at the piece of paper, perplexed by the swift return of her offer of food to the big bear upstairs. "Not hungry," was all it said.

Not hungry, her ass. She knew what a hungry bear looked like, and Gaius looked ravenous pretty much every time she saw him. Well, that'd teach him to turn down her food. She wasn't likely to make the offer again if he intended to disregard it out of hand.

She removed the plate and the note from the dumbwaiter and set it on the kitchen island, confident it wouldn't go to waste. Not two seconds later, Levi buzzed in, filled with more energy than a hummingbird.

"Ig wants to know if your last list of kitchen equipment is final. He's approving orders for all of it today. Oh hey, what's this?" His attention immediately diverted to the burger.

"Your lunch, if you want it," Nessa said, waving at the food.

"Sweet! Thanks, Ness!" She'd barely given him the go-ahead before the lanky young man grabbed the burger and inhaled half of it before she could blink.

While he chewed, his eyes settled on the scribbled note on the countertop. He pointed a potato wedge at it. "Gaius?"

Nessa nodded and Levi chuckled. "Dumbass. His loss!" He grinned around the last bite of burger.

She chuckled at his enthusiasm and was nearly bowled over when he gave her a peck on the cheek with more hearty "thanks" before charging back out the door, leaving her dizzy.

A second later, he ducked back in with a question about to pop from his mouth.

"The list is final," Nessa said. Levi nodded, smiled, and was off again in a blur.

She washed his empty dish, a little disappointed that Gaius hadn't accepted her gift. It made no sense, but apparently the man had an issue with her. She just hoped it wouldn't affect his work. She trusted Ignazio's opinion of the man's skill. If he was the professional her friend made him out to be, it shouldn't make a difference. But she wasn't going to waste precious energy trying to win the guy over if he was going to be so damned stubborn about accepting her friendship.

She remained aloof to him after that, merely commenting on his work each day in as neutral a way as possible. She couldn't help but be excited at the progress he was making. By the end of the week, the cabinets and sinks were installed and the pantry was close to completion. He had enlisted Levi's help laying tile after the energetic shifter ran out of garden work to help her with.

The afternoons were far too hot to work outdoors, though, so she retreated to the old kitchen that was as cool and dark as a cave, with chilled air flowing through from the ventilation ducts. She also felt the need to wallow in sentimental memories down here as much as possible. All too soon this old sanctuary would be torn down and replaced by Ig and Bry's rehab center. More white tile and stainless steel, if the plans were any indication.

Nessa was a little at a loss this afternoon. She'd finished cleaning up after lunch, and the boys had some kind of weekend-long event they were attending for League Champions, so she had no particular dinner obligations. It was still early afternoon and too hot to garden, but too nice a day to waste holed up with her memories.

She quirked her mouth at the dumbwaiter that sat idle, having only been used the one time for the rejected meal she'd sent to Gaius. Now was as good a time as any for him to tear the thing out.

And who the hell knew? Maybe after a week, the surly old bear had managed to cool off some and get used to her.

She hung up her apron in the pantry and headed outside where the heat blasted her hard enough to make sweat instantly pool between her breasts. She eyed the serene surface of the lake, thinking she ought to take a dip later. Bry and Ig's event lasted the full weekend, so she was off the hook for meals. After a week of their long-missed banter, she wasn't quite sure what to do with herself for an entire two days off. Probably work more on the garden and swim, and spend more time in her dad's old kitchen cooking her own favorite meals instead of the ones on her boss' special diet.

When she got up to the new kitchen, it was unexpectedly devoid of the sounds of hammers or power tools. She found Levi washing his hands in the big sink and the tilework was finished, but one of her countertop slabs was leaning against the wall and the other was nowhere to be seen. And of course, the dumbwaiter was still there when Gaius had promised he'd get to it by the end of the week.

"Where the hell is he?" she said.

Levi's head snapped up and he gave her a shocked look. "Who?"

"Gaius. What the hell happened to his stupid schedule? He said he'd have this stuff done. I need him to tear out that dumbwaiter when I'm not cooking."

"Don't know," Levi said with a shrug. "He just got all irritable and grumbly. He isn't exactly the most articulate guy, you may have noticed. Next thing I knew, he said something about 'finish if you want, I'll pay you double' and was gone. I don't think he realized that Ig's the one paying me."

"Dammit! I need him to at least get rid of that stupid . . . thing!" she pointed at the dumbwaiter, offended by its very presence.

"You can go *ask* him what's up, if it's that important to you. He lives just a few miles up the mountain." Levi pointed out the door toward the lushly-forested peaks that loomed behind the house.

"I think I will. Which way do I go?"

"Take a left out the driveway and keep going uphill until you see a big wooden gate with the Blackpaw emblem. Go through that gate and his is the only place. You can't miss it."

She thanked him and stormed out the doors, the heat only adding to her irritation.

"Nessa!" Levi called after her.

"What?" she snapped, ready to get on her way to tell the big bear she didn't appreciate his attitude. If he was going to bitch at her about interrupting his schedule, he should have the courtesy to stick to it himself.

"You want the keys to the spare transport?" She turned back in time to see him toss the keys to her.

"Thanks, Levi. You're the best."

CHAPTER
EIGHT
NESSA

Once she shut the gate behind her, Nessa's irritation subsided into curiosity. The higher she went into the mountains, the more intrigued she became about the bear who lived in such a remote corner of Astreia.

Even more curious was the structure that came into view as she rounded a bend in the road. She wouldn't call it a house, exactly, though it certainly had potential. She could make out the raw elegance of the architecture of what was likely to become a beautiful mountain cabin whenever it was finished. It was a sprawling, two-story structure that hugged the steep slope of the mountain like a mama dragon protecting her nest. But at the moment, it was no more than a skeleton with a very nice porch. An upper story had been built with a roof, at least, and a big stone chimney jutted out from the peak. The house had no real walls to speak of—just empty space that she could see all the way through to a spectacular waterfall beyond.

She parked the transport next to the other small transport in the gravel driveway and got out.

"Gaius!" she called, not wanting to surprise him if he was busy.

She stood in the driveway, marveling at the sturdy construction of the front porch for a moment before slowly venturing up the wide steps when nobody answered. The steps were flanked by a pair of massive posts that had been intricately carved with patterns she recognized as belonging to one of Astreia's oldest and most prestigious Northern bear clans, and at the top was the same emblem she'd seen on the gate: the big, stylized bear paw symbol for one of Astreia's most famous Champions. She ran her hand over the smooth ridges of the design, intrigued. He really must be a huge fan of the sport.

The rest of the house was only intriguing in its overwhelming potential. The interior was an entirely bare, open space with afternoon sunlight streaming through its empty framework, broken only by the massive stone fireplace that took up the very center. One corner was occupied by a single folding chair with a half-empty liquor bottle on the rough wood floor beside it. The chair faced what would likely be a picture window facing the most spectacular view of the lake someday, if the owner ever decided to finish the thing.

Nessa passed through the empty lower floor to the rear of the house and finally found signs of its missing occupant.

"Gaius!" she called again as she inspected the gorgeous rear deck that was clearly where the man had poured most of his inspiration so far. It butted up against the tree-covered hillside, with benches lining the uphill edge and railings along the side that overlooked the valley below. The corner closest to the house sported a sheltered area that had a quaint, but impressively outfitted outdoor kitchen, with a finished chopping block counter, a sink, a fridge, and a stone oven with a chimney that passed through the overhang above.

Smoke flowed gently from the chimney up into the vivid blue sky. A clothesline was the only thing that obscured the view, strung diagonally from the corner of the kitchen shelter to the far corner of the railing with laundry pinned to it and occasionally fluttering in the hot, barely there breeze.

The other side of the deck sported a big stone fire pit nestled low into the wooden planks. Fresh logs were already piled up inside it, ready to be lit. Another folding chair rested beside it.

Unable to restrain herself, Nessa opened his fridge and peered inside. She chuckled when she found a plate with a pair of perfectly constructed meat patties, and another with sliced vegetables and cheese. On the counter was a bowl covered with a damp towel. As expected, the bowl contained a dark, yeast-scented globe of rising bread dough.

"So you're definitely a chef in your own right . . . but where the hell are you?" she murmured, looking around and frowning.

The deck extended farther toward the waterfall. Nessa wandered to the edge and peered over, gasping at the steep drop-off that ended in a deliciously deep and refreshing-looking pool fed by the waterfall. Following the railing, she found another set of steps that led down to a wide landing overlooking another section of the pool. Here there was a hammock stretched between two posts, holding what appeared to be rolled-up bedding and a pillow.

Even more curious about the big man, she continued down, following the deck that descended two more landings to a perfect open dock hanging over the water.

There she finally caught a glimpse of him, his big, tattooed torso half-concealed on the far side of the swimming hole, submerged beneath the heavy torrent of water plunging from high above. She cupped her hands around her mouth and called his name again, but the crash of the waterfall drowned out her voice.

She huffed and put her hands on her hips. The water looked so damn nice, the coolness of it already breaking through the summer heat where she stood. No wonder he'd come home and gone for a swim. She'd been about to do the exact same thing before she came up here, intent on nagging him as if he was some ungrateful, wayward child.

Her craving for a taste of that cool water destroyed her desire to complain. So what if it took an extra day before her kitchen was done? That just meant she'd have more time to spend in the old space, reminiscing.

Rather than attempt another futile yell over the noise of the water, she simply stripped, tearing off her shirt and shorts until she was naked. Then she stepped back several feet and made a run for the edge, whooping with joy as she dove off in a graceful arc and plunged beneath the crisp mountain water.

CHAPTER NINE

GAIUS

Gaius tensed at what sounded for all the world like a Champion's battle cry echoing through his private cove. Then a splash behind him made him spin around and nearly slip off the big rock he'd been sitting on while waiting for the swelling in his knees to subside.

He slid off the rock anyway and swam a few feet toward the ripples left in the surface by whoever had just joined him. The dark head that emerged a few seconds later made him do a double-take.

Nessa's clear bell of a laugh rang through the cove, her brown eyes bright with elation. "This place is *amazing*! How dare you hoard it for yourself?" She swam in a slow arc and then rolled over to stretch onto her back, her gaze drifting around the cove from the waterfall to the dock and over his half-finished house.

Gaius' gaze, however, fixed on the perfect globes of her breasts emerging from the surface of the water, brown nipples tight and pebbled from the cold. His blood rushed south and his previously cold-shrunk cock swelled to full hardness.

Fucking hell, of course it had to be her.

More irritated than aroused, despite whatever ideas his stupid pecker had, he groused at her. "Not hoarding it. It's just half-finished." Which should've been obvious. "Half-finished" was being rather generous, in fact.

"Why the hell not? This place is perfect. Gaius, you've been seriously holding out on me. What other secrets have you got?"

"Why are you here?" he asked, treading water and hoping his enormous hard-on wasn't visible from her angle.

Far too enthralled by his house and property, Nessa turned and began a slow backstroke in the other direction. This time, she swam about two feet directly in front of him, giving him a tantalizing view of the entire length of her deliciously curvy body, from her light brown shoulders all the way to the dark triangle of silken curls between her legs. Even though he'd seen most of her in the skimpy shorts and top she wore while gardening, he'd had no concept of how beautifully graceful she could be. She was like some lost water nymph come to seduce him.

He shook his head when she said something and realized he hadn't heard a word she'd said for the last several seconds. Then her words registered. "At first I came to find out why you left a whole pile of things unfinished..."

His teeth involuntarily clenched. "Had I known you'd come all the way up here just to gripe at me, I could've saved you the trip," he snapped, surging past her with long sweeps of his arms through the water. He didn't hear the rest of whatever she said through the water in his ears. When he made it to the dock, he grabbed the ladder and hauled himself up, shook himself off, then stomped up the steps to the main deck.

His cock was still hard. He stopped and stared down at the traitorous appendage, then shook his head in irritation. Pacing across the deck, he scrubbed his hands over his head, struggling to tamp down the whirlwind of conflicting unwelcome feelings—anger at her for invading his space, and desire and arousal for wanting her there for more than just simple company.

The fact was he'd been lonely for a long time. It had been so long since he'd retired and made that call to the matchmaker Oracle he'd concluded that he was a lost cause. And now this perfectly gorgeous, yet utterly infuriating woman had walked into his life, and he wasn't sure if he wanted to *kick* her out or *fuck her brains* out.

One thing he knew was that Nessa was the perfect example of the kind of woman he *didn't* want. She was just too damn bossy and downright exasperating. He was retired now, making a job out of what had been a beloved hobby in his past. This was when he was supposed to *relax*. Find a mate he could settle down with. Not be set upon at every turn by a woman whose life's work seemed to be to get his blood boiling.

Still pacing, he caught a glimpse of her climbing out of the water, all tantalizing wet curves and long, sleek hair draped over her shoulders. She looked so soft everywhere, his palms just itched to . . .

"Fuck!" he yelled, scrubbing his hands through his hair again to dispel that urge. He took a deep breath and was gratified to see his cock had finally gotten the hint that he *wasn't* intending to fuck Nessa.

When he turned again, she was coming up the steps with an irritated look, still naked and holding a dripping bundle in her arms.

Suddenly overwhelmed by modesty, he darted to his

clothesline and snatched a dry towel, slinging it hurriedly around his waist.

When she came up the last few steps, he prepared a litany of complaints to throw at her, but found himself struck dumb yet again by the beauty who stood defiantly in front of him. Holy fuck, was she gorgeous when she was pissed.

"You fucking *soaked* my clothes, you big oaf!" she snapped, holding out one of the sodden pieces of fabric she was carrying and wringing it out to demonstrate. "I don't suppose you have a clothes dryer up in this unfinished shell you call a house? No? Didn't think so." She glared daggers at him, and if his cock hadn't already gone soft, he was sure that look would've done the job—if she hadn't been naked while giving it to him.

He'd barely shaken his head and formed a response when she stomped over to his clothesline. "I guess they'll just have to dry the old fashioned way," she said, pinning the garments to the cable where his other laundry swung in the warm breeze. "I'm going to borrow this while I wait," she added, snatching one of his favorite old flannel work shirts and shrugging into it.

Gaius blinked at her as she fastened the buttons, unsure of how to respond. He couldn't argue with her. He'd been the ass who shaken water all over her clothes in his need to escape.

And now that she was dressed in nothing but an ancient, threadbare shirt of his, he was somehow completely disarmed. Perhaps it was the fact that her *goods* were safely hidden away and he could finally cool down enough to think. Before, she'd been all sexy-as-sin curves and wet, bronze skin. Now she was decidedly less intimidating in a shirt that was three sizes too big. She was *still* rolling up the sleeves, and the hem nearly reached her knees.

"Sorry," he finally managed, though his timing was so off he may as well have been apologizing for the size of the shirt.

"It'll do," she said, her lips quirking into a sweet smile, which slowly bled into a chuckle.

Perplexed at first, he frowned at her. Then the absurdity of the situation hit him and he laughed. "You just help yourself to my closet, Nessa. Don't mind me."

After her melodic giggle subsided, she eyed him up and down and said, "You look better naked, anyway." Then, after the briefest pause, she added, "Were those fresh burgers I saw in your fridge? I admit I'd like a taste of whatever it is that made you think *my* offering wasn't good enough to touch your lips."

Gaius chuckled and bent his head, rubbing his mouth to dispel the tingling that'd overtaken his lips. "You saw right. I've, ah, got more than enough meat, if you're hungry."

He darted a glance at her with a hesitant quirk to his mouth and was gratified to see a sparkle in her eyes. Nope, she was no shrinking violet, this one.

"I noticed," she said. "I could eat." Then she stepped back and waved him to his outdoor kitchen.

With a nod, he tightened his towel around his hips and moved toward the stone oven. Squatting, he opened the fire box and jabbed at the coals with a poker, then added a couple logs to the heat. It was about right for the buns. While they got going, he'd start the fire pit for the burgers to grill on.

He made it halfway to standing when pain blasted through his right knee, then through his left, so excruciating he cursed and gripped the edge of the countertop to steady himself. Claws shot from his fingers, digging into the hard wood beneath, a reflex born of old training still ingrained after three decades as a Champion.

"Shit, what's wrong?" Nessa said, darting to his side. "Did you burn yourself?"

She rested a gentle hand on his arm that somehow managed to clear his head the tiniest bit. Gritting his teeth, he shook his head.

"Nah. Old injury. It pains me worse in humid weather. The falls usually help if I soak long enough. 'S one of the reasons I bought this land."

"Here, let me help you sit," she said. Without waiting for a reply, she slipped an arm around his waist and grabbed his wrist, tucking her head beneath his elbow. Before he could process her request, she had him supported against her softness and was leading him toward the fire pit.

He groaned as she lowered him into his chair, and was dimly grateful that the pair of hot coals that had taken up residence in his knee joints distracted his cock enough that it stayed flaccid beneath his towel.

Nessa squatted in front of him with a worried look. "Where does it hurt?" she asked, peering up into his eyes.

"Knees," he bit out, gripping them and squeezing. "I've got a bit of salve in the fridge. And the liquor . . . that's around here somewhere."

"Just sit, I've got you," Nessa said with a soft smile. Gaius nodded and smiled back, his gaze inadvertently drifting down the open collar of her shirt. He silently thanked whatever gods existed for the lost buttons. The old thing had gradually lost half its buttons to the point he had to remove the top ones and sew them back on at the bottom just to make the garment halfway serviceable. He pretty much only wore it working on his own house now. But after seeing her in it, he doubted he'd ever wear the thing again.

When she stood and went back to the fridge, he took a deep breath, admiring the way her full, round backside flexed beneath the tail of his shirt. Nope, it definitely belonged on her.

Fuck, what was he thinking? Not half an hour ago he was cursing her very existence. But he couldn't deny she was a sweetheart, despite her ongoing inclination to get under his skin.

At least now her sympathy seemed to have overridden any particular need to torment him with her demands.

Nessa opened the fridge and bent over to peer inside. Gaius let out a soft growl as the hem of his shirt rode up her thighs, baring the curved creases of the underside of her ass. Just an inch more and he'd have a view even more spectacular than the mountains and the lake outside his front window. He bit his lip, hoping. She was at least easy on the eyes, even if she was a test to his patience.

But alas, she found his medicine and stood again. As she turned she sniffed it and grimaced. "How old is this stuff? Does it even work anymore?"

"I made it a few weeks ago. That was before the humidity kicked up for the summer, though."

"These herbs grow in your woods?"

"Yeah, but . . ." Before he could finish the thought, she'd tossed his salve in the trash and run off toward the woods. By the time he turned to call after her, all he saw was the dark, fur-covered backside of a she-bear and his shirt hanging on a branch at the edge of the deck.

Gaius could hear her rustling around in the woods behind the house, her bear's telltale chuffing sounds a sign that she was in the midst of dedicated searching for the healing herbs. He shook his head and laughed to himself, amused by how focused she was on a goal once she got it into her head.

Eventually the sounds came closer and he sat back, smiling and waiting. Then it came . . . the pause near the other side of the house followed by the sound of running and then an exclaimed "Oh!" from a now apparently human-shaped Nessa. She'd found his garden.

Several minutes later, she came padding barefoot around the section of deck that stretched between the side of the house and the hillside. Gaius restrained himself from looking until she came into view and set down a big basket loaded with greenery. He exhaled slowly at the sight of her, his entire body warming as he took in her naked shape, savoring those last few seconds before she covered up again with his shirt.

All he really needed was the sight of her and the pain disappeared, but that was a recipe for disaster if he gave in. Not only was she a headstrong, infuriating woman, but from the look of her, she was far too young for him anyway.

Still, he had no compunctions against enjoying the view while he could. At least now that they'd crossed the barrier of seeing each other naked, it didn't rile him up so much.

She turned and carried the basket across the deck to the outdoor kitchen. "Why didn't you tell me you had a whole garden full of the stuff?"

"I would've, if you'd listened. You seem to tune out once you get an idea into your head." He leaned forward and rubbed his knees, the throbbing ache returning now that the magical diversion of Nessa's naked body had disappeared.

His soft hiss caught her attention and she said, "Oh, I almost forgot." Holding up a finger, she jogged into the house and came back a moment later with his bottle of liquor, along with his other chair.

"Until I get your salve made," she said, handing the bottle to him, then setting the chair on the opposite side of his fire pit.

"You are a goddamn angel," Gaius said. He took a swig and sat back, letting the pleasant buzz of the alcohol numb his pain while he watched her work. She was mesmerizing. So sure and confident. He wondered if he could amend his request to the matchmaker and ask for a woman like Nessa, just a little older and a lot less overbearing. He was enough of a control freak himself—he needed a woman who was willing to compromise.

Yet somehow he didn't mind when he realized she'd taken the liberty of making the rolls for the burgers and slid them into the oven, then came over and expertly lit the fire in the pit in front of him.

Finally, she retrieved the bowl where she'd left the crushed herbs to steep and came over to kneel in front of him. Gaius sat up, swallowing in surprise at the sudden closeness of her.

Nessa laughed. "I'm not going to bite. You're in pain, and it's better if you don't try to obliterate it entirely with that bottle." She nodded toward the liquor he held loosely on his towel-covered lap. She gently extracted it from his grip and set it on the deck beside his chair. "Now, let me see your knees."

Gaius dropped his hands to the arms of the chair, forcing himself to remain aloof while she pushed his towel up his thighs a few inches to reveal both his damaged, swollen joints. She winced.

"Yeah, that bad," he said.

"What the hell did you do to yourself?" she asked. She

pushed his legs farther apart, forcing him to drop his hands and bunch the towel between his legs to avoid giving her a peek at his assets when she bent to inspect the pair of matching scars that lined the inside of each knee.

"Old arena injuries, that's all."

Nessa's brows shot up. "You're a Champion?"

"Was. Retired about two years ago. These old things just couldn't take it anymore."

Nessa looked at his knees and then back up at him, her gaze almost reverent as though some amazing revelation had come to her. "You're the Blackpaw, aren't you?"

It was Gaius' turn to be surprised. "Little before your time, don't you think?"

With a shrug, she settled down on her haunches and reached into the bowl, withdrawing a long, sheer piece of bandage that was soaked through with the viscous golden liquid. "My dad followed your career. He was a big fan. Even though I think he disagreed with what you did."

Gaius snorted. That was typical of his generation of bears. You simply didn't give up clan leadership if there was any choice in the matter.

He jumped when she gripped his calf and urged him to straighten his leg.

"Seriously, settle down. You're making *me* jumpy. So, tell me why you did it."

He stretched out his leg allowing her to rest his foot on her thigh. When she leaned over, the underside of her breast grazed his big toe through the fabric of his shirt. But the brief, charged sensation was nothing compared to the relief that seeped into his leg when she started wrapping the medicine-infused bandage around his knee.

"You don't even ask, you just demand, don't you?"

Nessa narrowed her gaze at him. "You don't have to

answer. I'm just curious. You could have been the Blackrock clan leader, but you let that go. Was it the fame or the money?"

"Neither. I just couldn't see myself in charge. I like my life how I like it. Stayed in the solo bracket too, despite hundreds of offers to join up with other Champions. Could've made more money in a duo or a trio. A Clan leader has thousands of people to answer to—they never get any peace. You may have noticed I like my solitude."

Her fingertips tickled his inner thigh as she wound the bandage higher, crisscrossing it over his joint for secure coverage. His belly warmed, and he was sure it wasn't from the several swallows of liquor he'd downed when she handed him his bottle. But it wasn't so much arousal as it was an odd sort of comfort at her gentle touch . . . something he hadn't felt in far too long.

She made a soft hum of understanding as she secured the bandage on one knee and shifted to his other leg. "My mom has this crazy dream that I'll wind up mated to a clan leader someday. I just humor her." She shook her head and pressed her lips together, her expression half irritated and half tender. "She means well, I know."

"You don't want that? It'd be good life—being a clan leader's mate."

Nessa tilted her head and quirked her mouth to the side, thinking. "It's not that I don't want it. I just want what I want, you know? And what I want right now is this job."

"Did you tell your mama that?"

"She knows, but she's stubborn too." She shot him a playful look. "It's just easier to let her do her thing and I'll do mine. I doubt that Oracle will ever find a man who'd tolerate me anyway. I mean, *you* seem like the nicest guy, but I can tell you don't like me. Somehow I manage to repel any men I didn't grow up with moments after meeting them. I think Ig and Bry and Levi are immune to whatever it is that turns off everyone else, which I'm grateful for."

Gaius frowned and started to protest, but she shot him a warning look. "Don't think I haven't caught onto your little grumbles whenever I walk into the room. It's all right, I'm used to it." She shrugged. "I just focus on the food and my friends. I'm happy enough."

But she didn't look happy in that moment. If anything, she looked close to tears. At a loss, Gaius reached down for the liquor bottle and offered it to her with raised eyebrows.

Nessa took it, nodded her thanks, then tilted it back and took a long swig. Her throat rippled as she swallowed, the long, golden column holding his attention as he followed the line of it down. As if succumbing to some strange gravitational pull, his gaze continued lower, down her chest to the crease of her cleavage visible between the edges of his shirt.

Again, his palms itched with the desire to feel both those gorgeous globes spilling out of his grip. When she handed the bottle back to him, he took another long drink —for courage, or strength, or just to numb himself, he wasn't sure anymore, but she was starting to get to him in a way he wasn't quite sure he was prepared for.

As quickly as her mood had darkened, it shifted again. She patted both his knees gently and gave him a brilliant smile, then hopped up.

"Alrighty then, let's see how these burgers of yours stand up to mine." With a wink, she turned and trotted back to the counter.

CHAPTER
TEN
GAIUS

Now that both his knees were wrapped, the pain had finally diminished to a dull ache that was slowly disappearing. Gaius finally had the presence of mind to do more than just sit and be waited on, so he shifted forward, grabbed the extra poker by the edge of the fire pit, and jabbed at the burning logs until they settled into a nice bed of glowing coals.

While he set up the grill, Nessa pulled the buns from the oven and set them out to cool. She bent into the fridge again and retrieved the pair of patties he'd made that morning, then grabbed the bowl of ground meat he'd planned to freeze for later. She made happy little humming sounds while she put together another pair of patties and carried them over.

"These smell delicious. Not a combination of spices I'd have chosen, but I can see why they'd work. How did you come up with this recipe? And more importantly, will you share it?"

He sat back and crossed his arms, grinning at her. "Hey, now. A man's got to have some secrets."

She rolled her eyes. "I can work it out easily enough on my own. Magic tongue." She stuck out her tongue and pointed at it as she handed him the plate and spatula. "You could blindfold me and I'd be able to tell you what's in a recipe. Like that swill you drink is bottom-shelf dreck. You need to talk to Ig about getting some better booze. He has the best sources."

He made a noncommittal noise. "It's medical. Medicine's not supposed to taste good or you'd never want to heal."

Nessa's mouth dropped open and her hand went to her chest as she gasped in mock offense. "My cooking has been proven to heal all ills. Why do you think Ig hired me? Pretty much every growing thing on Astreia has some kind of medicinal property, if you know how to unlock it."

Gaius had heard about the new diet trend that had become popular among the Arena Champions over the past couple years. He hadn't realized his friends had fallen for it, though. He grunted at her, shaking his head.

"You don't believe me? Give me two weeks. Eat what I cook for you every day and I guarantee your old injuries will never bother you again."

"Not sure I want to agree to you bossing me around any more than necessary," he said.

"I'm not bossy!" she said with a hurt look. "I'm just usually right. There's a difference. I also don't enjoy seeing my friends hurting. Give it a shot . . . best case, you wind up more mobile than you've been, without pain. Worst case, you get fed. How can you go wrong?" She smiled sunnily at him, and he couldn't help but smile back.

"Fair enough. Now move your sweet behind so I can get this meat grilling." He shooed her out of his way and bent to put the burgers on the grill. Nessa trotted around the fire pit and planted herself in the other chair, sighing in relaxation as she stared around at his little sanctuary, such as it was.

They sat in silence, nothing but the occasional pop of the coals, the sizzle of the meat, and the steady drone of the falls filling the space between.

Every so often he'd glance up at her, expecting her to ask more uninvited questions or offer some unsolicited opinion, yet she seemed perfectly content to just watch him cook or gaze off down the valley.

The pair of Astreia suns had finally begun to descend, so the air was at least comfortable as opposed to blazing. It was easily the most peaceful time of day up here, and without the nagging pain in his knees, Gaius felt about as content as Nessa looked. The feeling was so foreign, he wasn't quite sure what to do with it.

In that moment, nothing much mattered. Not his aged, beat-up Champion's body, not his half-finished, half-baked skeleton of a house, not his failure at finding a mate despite hiring an Oracle with a flawless record that cost him a pretty penny. All that mattered was the peace and quiet and the prospect of a delicious supper. Having a beautiful woman to share it with, who he decided was probably better company than he'd originally thought, was just a bonus.

When the burgers finished cooking, Nessa rose without speaking to build them, then returned with two plates. Gaius waited for a moment before taking a bite, curious to see her reaction first.

Nessa opened her mouth and sank her teeth in, crunching through the pile of greens and condiments she'd added before topping the thing with a fresh-baked bun. Her pretty brown eyes fluttered closed, and she let out such a moan of pure pleasure his cock hardened fully for the first time since he'd watched her naked body floating past him in the water.

His mouth went completely dry, and he couldn't tear his eyes away from watching her eat for several seconds. Finally, she licked her lips and exclaimed, "My *god*, this is amazing. Everything about it. Where did you learn to cook like this?"

Shaking himself back to awareness, Gaius held his plate solidly over his hard-on and shrugged. "Always believed it's best to specialize. Focus on that one thing you want to perfect. In the arena, I was the best grappling fighter there was. With building, kitchens are my specialty, though I'm damn good at everything else when it comes to wood. And I've cooked for myself for a long time . . . long enough to perfect at least one meal. And this is it."

"Mmm, good philosophy," she said. "Where'd you pick up this recipe? It's not that common on Astreia. You spend much time on Earth?"

"Only about a month every summer. Spent a little longer there after I retired. Had to get away to gather my thoughts. Make a plan. You know." He nodded at Nessa as if she'd have any idea what he meant. She was barely out of the cradle, and while his career as a Champion had been cut short due to his injuries, he'd still been part of that scene for two decades.

"How many summers, exactly?" she asked, idly glancing at him as she sopped up the last juices from her second burger with the remainder of her bun. He sensed she was digging for his age and decided to settle that debate.

"I'm a lot older than you, Ness. Maybe not as old as your dad, but old enough."

"Old enough to be a cranky old bear? Old enough to hide from the world in a half-finished cabin? Old enough..."

"Old enough to value my peace and quiet," he grumbled, cutting her off.

Nessa snorted and stood up, retrieved his plate, and carried their dishes to the sink, where she washed them both and set them in the rack to dry. She really had made herself at home, and he abstractly wondered if she'd be at home in any kitchen. Then he thought probably not as at home as she'd seemed in the old kitchen at Ig's. Something about that particular kitchen fit her in a way he couldn't put his finger on.

"Sounds like a recipe for loneliness," she quipped. "Was that part of the plan you made when you retired? Because you seem intent on hiding from the world up here." She leaned against the counter and crossed her arms, then tilted her chin at the house. "And as nice as your place is, it sure seems like an empty life you're living."

His shoulders fell and he scrubbed his hands through his hair, then tugged on his beard. "No, that wasn't the plan. I met with an Oracle matchmaker when I visited Earth right after I retired. It's been two years since. But it wasn't like I didn't try. Figure she must know something I don't."

"That you're a pain in the ass? That Oracle's no doubt got your number on that count," she said, grinning at him. "But that'd make two of us. My mom met with an Oracle when I was a baby... a fucking *baby*... hoping that if she got ahead of things, she could land me a clan leader's son for a mate. If an actual Oracle can't find *me* a guy in all that time, either they're not as infallible as we think, or you and I really are both lost causes."

"Thought you said you didn't want to be a clan leader's mate," Gaius said.

"I don't! But that doesn't mean I don't like the idea of knowing there's a match out there for me. That someone—even if it's a mystical dolphin shifter who's maybe too manipulative for her own good—believes I'm good enough to be matched with someone like that."

"Ever think maybe *you're* too good?" Gaius asked, then mentally kicked himself. She already had a big enough ego.

Nessa laughed, the sound ringing clear and bright over the rush of the waterfall. The suns were lower in the sky, their light streaming through beneath the outdoor kitchen's overhang and glinting off Nessa's silky black hair. It had dried in soft waves that looked every bit as decadent to touch as the rest of her.

"All right. That earns you a few points of forgiveness for all the grouchy things you usually spit at me. Why don't you give me a tour of your house? I want to hear about this plan of yours."

She started for the door without waiting and Gaius got up to follow, somehow drawn to her demand despite having little to nothing to actually say. She wandered through the rear of the house first, then paused in one corner of the empty space, looking at him expectantly. "Well?"

"My plan was to use my Arena winnings to buy this land and build a house. That's kind of the whole story."

"So . . . how long has it been since you started this? That garden out there's got perennials that are at least a year old."

"Two years ago, the summer before I retired. I laid the foundation and built the fireplace that summer. Planted the garden and built the deck, too. Put up the frame and... well, most of what you see now I did last year."

She put her hands on her hips and gave him a hard look. "A year. You've been living in this empty shell for *a year*."

Gaius pressed his lips together and glanced out at the deck where the flames flickered in the fire pit.

Nessa rolled her eyes when he returned his gaze to her. "Yeah, okay, you live on your porch, but why haven't you finished this place? You must have had a plan for it when you started."

He swallowed and gave her a helpless look. "I didn't expect to have to finish it alone," he muttered, unwilling to share more of his original pipe dream. He'd hoped the Oracle would come through and that he and his future mate would merge their dreams into the house. The longer he waited, the harder it became to envision anything but the bare necessities—which he already had outside.

Nessa dropped her hands and stepped toward him. She gave him a gentle pat on the shoulder. "Well, you aren't alone now. Let's see what we can do to inspire you to finish."

She trotted off to another corner of the empty space, near what was supposed to be the front door. He hadn't even gotten around to framing out interior walls yet. So far he'd only built a frame for the front door and a few windows—the ones that he thought had the best views. Neither of those were about the interior of the house so much as the place where it was built. The windows were situated to capture the spectacular sunrises and sunsets over the Astreia mountains and the lake nestled in the valley. At the moment, the interior was as empty of inspiration as his cold, dead heart.

He heard Nessa let out a soft exclamation somewhere

beyond the massive stone fireplace he'd built in the very center of the house. He followed with a few cautious steps, tightening his towel around his hips and kicking himself for not putting on actual pants.

He found her at the western corner, staring out at the sunset. "This is the living room," she said, with utter certainty. "You're keeping an open floor plan, right? So you don't really need any walls, just to finish it. But this is *definitely* the living room. It gets the best afternoon light, and you've already got a dual fireplace, so one side's got to be the living room anyway. This is it."

She went on to describe in more detail why it was perfect, and by the time she was finished, Gaius could easily envision the space that way, with a huge, comfortable sofa facing the fireplace on one side and the windows on the other.

"Dining room here," she said, returning the way she'd come. She gazed up at the high, vaulted ceiling. He'd built the second floor in a loft style, intending to leave half the upper story open, with high windows across the front of the house facing the mountain view where Astreia's twin suns rose in the mornings.

She navigated around the piles of lumber he'd stacked against the dormant fireplace, along with his tools and other sundries, then went for the stairwell in the corner.

"I've got to see that view from upstairs," she said.

Gaius started up behind her and stopped with his foot on the first step as he caught a perfect view of her bare backside peeking out from under the hem of his shirt. He stood mesmerized for a moment before shaking himself and raking a hand through his hair. She was far too much of a temptation for an old bear like him.

But as he ascended the first few steps without a single

twinge of pain in his knees, he started to wonder if maybe he'd been wrong about her. Bossy, she may be . . . but she sure knew her shit when it came to herbs. Not even his own concoction of salves had given him this much relief, despite following the recipe his Arena League doctor had given him. Unless it really was just the sight of her naked backside that obliterated all his senses.

He chuckled to himself. There could be worse ways to feel no pain.

The sight of Nessa's pretty face bathed in the warm glow of the brilliant Astreia sunset was another way to forget the pain. She stood at the far edge of the second floor, leaning on the railing of the deck and staring out at the view, completely enraptured. When he ascended the last few steps, her focus shifted to him, yet somehow that look of awestruck amazement remained, making him feel for all the world like it was *him* she was amazed by.

"You really are a master," she said. "This place is perfect. Every single inch."

For the briefest moment, her gaze skittered down his big frame and back up before she let out a little sigh and redirected her focus to the view outside.

He came up beside her and leaned on the rail, propping both his forearms across it. His shoulder brushed hers, and she seemed to lean into him the slightest bit. She smelled like woodsmoke from the fire, but underneath was the softest hint of nutmeg.

"How could you *not* be inspired by this view? I mean, look at that!" She waved her arm at the expanse of gilded sky, her face practically glowing with awe.

Gaius shot a cursory glance at the vista he'd chosen this land for, then looked back at her. "Maybe I just needed someone to share it with," he said, giving her a bump with his shoulder.

"Well, it would be a shame for you to hoard it all to yourself. Anytime you want to share, you let me know." She turned around, surveying the open space behind them. It was almost too dim to see much, but there wasn't much to see anyway.

"This one's a no-brainer. Bedroom. But you've got to leave it open to the view from the east, too. Morning sun, and all. Do you plan on having kids if the matchmaker ever hooks you up?"

She shot him a quick glance as she passed by toward the stairs again. Surprised by her question, he followed without answering at first. Nessa stopped at the top step and looked back at him. "Not part of your plan?"

"No . . . I mean, yeah. That was always the hope. There's more than enough room on the first floor for a couple more bedrooms."

"Good," she said, trotting back down with an eager, skipping, stride. She stopped at the very center of the first floor in front of the cathedral-style window he'd framed out. This one faced east. She grinned as he strolled in.

"So, what's your vision here? Den? Torture chamber?" he asked.

She shook her head. "Not even close. This is the heart of the house. Don't tell me you don't already know what belongs here. With that view to the east, there's only one thing . . ."

"Kitchen," he said, then laughed. "You are one amazing woman, Nessa. One-track mind, too."

"Aw, I wouldn't say that." Her eyes darted to his hips and she gave him a coy smile before launching into the most intricate description of the perfect kitchen. By the end of it, he had yet another image in his head that even outdid the living room in its elaborate detail. But what he saw in his mind's eye was almost a perfect recreation of the old kitchen in Ig's house, minus the cave-like quality.

"Instead of a wall, you'd build a bar counter between the kitchen and the dining room so the morning light reaches all the way through. Or better yet, just keep the dining room in that corner and add sliding doors that open completely for an outdoor dining room in the summer. Then this view won't go to waste no matter what time of day you're in here."

She continued walking in a circle to trace out the boundaries of the room. For a split-second, Gaius had the most vivid image of not only the kitchen she'd just described to him, but her cooking in it. Along with that image came the memory of all the scents he'd endured over the past week, wafting up the dumbwaiter shaft he'd neglected to cover up after that first day.

He'd halfway hoped she'd make him another peace offering, but she hadn't, which had lent to his grouchiness, though nowhere near as much as the increasing ache in his damaged knees.

An unbearable ache of a different sort took up residence in his chest, a craving to make that vision real. But that was as ridiculous an idea as Nessa's mom's insistence on getting her hitched to a clan leader, sight unseen.

Still, as she grew quiet and thoughtful, the ache persisted. She wandered over to the framed out window and leaned against the open windowsill. It had grown dark while they made their tour, but the space was well-illuminated from the rising moon peeking over the tops of the trees to the east.

Nessa stared out at it with another wistful sigh that

made Gaius' chest tighten with the need to ease whatever sadness had overtaken her. He moved up behind her and rested a hand on her shoulder.

"There's nothin' to be sad about with a view like that," he said, giving her a little squeeze. To his surprise, she rested her hand atop his and squeezed back, then leaned back against him. She let out a soft hum as though drawing strength from his sturdy presence. He reflexively dropped his hands to her hips and rested his chin on top of her head.

"No. That view is probably the second-best thing about this place."

He nodded, though she couldn't see. "You're right, the falls are what caught my eye first." He squeezed her a little tighter, enjoying the way her small, soft body fit against him and hoping to offer whatever comfort she seemed to be asking for with that lean into him.

Nessa shook her head. "The falls are just part of the view." She twisted her head around against his shoulder and peered up at him. "The best part is you."

Gaius' heart stopped beating.

CHAPTER ELEVEN

NESSA

The big, gruff bear froze, his blue gaze fixed on Nessa's upturned face. Her heart pounded so hard she worried she might faint if he didn't respond. She'd taken a leap, but it was no lie. Gaius' half-built house had vision, but somewhere along the way, he'd lost it. There was no mistaking his original intention with the way he'd focused the basic design on the surroundings. It just proved how aware he was of his environment, yet he'd forgotten about the most important part of his plan.

His heart. His heart had clearly been in the game when he'd chosen this site and started building, but for whatever reason, that part of him had lost interest. There was only so far she could go with her ideas to jump-start his interest in finishing. The rest had to come from him. And despite her conviction that she wasn't the future mate he'd envisioned, she wanted to be there to see this place completed, to see him happy in it.

Maybe it was selfish of her to want this. The more she'd seen, the more she wished this place could be part of *her* dream as much as it had been his at the start. Everything about it called to some deep part of her as much as Ig's offer of a position on his staff had screamed, "This is your future!"

Gaius didn't really want her for the long-term; he'd made that clear. But she'd be happy to see him through even the short-term, if it meant being able to see this place's potential fully realized.

But when he closed the distance between them and his mouth found hers, her desire found its true target. It wasn't the house at all that she wanted. It was the man who was building it.

And oh, god, did she want him.

He tightened his arm around her waist and lifted his other hand to cup her face, tilting his mouth across hers to deepen the kiss. She moaned into him when his tongue swept deep, sliding hot and wet against her own, as though he craved a taste of her every bit as much as she'd wanted a taste of him.

He slipped his hand lower, grazing his fingertips across her collarbone and down the center of her chest. With his index finger, he hooked the fastened button between her breasts and slipped it open, then slid his hand inside and cupped her heavy breast. His thumb grazed her nipple and she gasped from the pleasure, breaking the kiss and turning back to the view as she arched into his touch.

He slipped his hand back out of her shirt and slowly unfastened the remaining buttons, dipping his head to graze his lips and teeth along the side of her neck.

Nessa's entire body quivered with a need she'd never felt in her life—the need to be devoured by one man, claimed and fully possessed to the point the rest of the world ceased to exist.

Gaius unfastened the last button and grazed his hands

up her belly to gently cup both her breasts. He growled low and deep as they filled his palms, and he thumbed her nipples in slow, tortuous circles.

She started to shrug out of the shirt, but he caught it and tugged it back up.

"I want you in this," he said, his voice low and rumbling so deep it vibrated down to her core. "Just this when you're here in my house."

He turned her in his arms and pulled the collar of the shirt up to her neck, fingering the threadbare fabric. The light contact against her neck sent little jolts of pleasure through her that grew more intense as he slipped his hands down the open sides and spread them around her bared breasts.

"Gaius . . ." His name emerged as a plea on her lips, though for what, she didn't know. He silenced her with his mouth, stooping to lift her and set her on the open windowsill.

She wrapped her arms around his neck and hooked her ankles behind his thighs to hold on. When he broke from the kiss, breathless, he reached back and unfastened her hands from his neck, then leaned away from her with his fingers twined in hers.

Gaius raked his gaze over her exposed body, her chest heaving from the need to catch her breath after the desperate hunger in their kiss. Moonlight from behind her caught the silver glinting in his beard and the hints of age-old longing in his eyes.

For what seemed like ages, he just stared at her, and she worried he'd come to his senses and decided cradle-robbing wasn't his thing. Then he smiled and said, "This is the view I was missing."

Then he was on her again, hungrily devouring her

mouth and moving lower. Nessa gasped as he wrapped his lips around one nipple, sucking while he kneaded her other breast. She tangled her fingers in his hair and tilted her head back with a groan, pushing against his hips when they pressed tight against her core, his length hard and urgent beneath his towel.

Anxious to feel his skin against hers, she dipped her fingertips into the twisted fabric beneath his navel and tugged. The towel unfurled and fell away from his hips, and instantly his searing heat slipped along the soaked channel between her thighs.

He let out another low, rumbling growl that echoed through the empty house. His hands left her breasts, dropping to her hips to yank her hard against him so her folds spread across the base of his shaft.

Nessa gasped from the abrupt pressure against her clit and the delicious slide of his thick length as he tilted his hips and grazed his cock along her tender flesh. He stared down between them, holding her legs wide while he slowly stroked his cock back and forth along her flooded channel.

He lifted his gaze to hers, the moonlight reflected in his eyes highlighting the hunger that blazed deep within him. There was only the hint of a question when he slid his cock down her channel again until the broad tip was nestled right at her opening. Her entire body throbbed with the need for him to follow through, yet he waited wordlessly.

Nessa's she-bear let out an impatient growl she was sure he'd heard. She translated the needy beast's message in case there was any misunderstanding: "Fuck me already!"

Gaius answered with a roar of his own as he plunged into her with one powerful stroke. He hooked a hand into her hair at the base of her skull and tilted her head back as he thrust hard into her. His teeth grazed the line of her throat, tongue licking and sucking at her sensitive skin and sending little jolts of ecstasy that all met at her core, fanning her flames hotter with each new touch.

She needed more of him, but had no leverage to get it where he had her poised on the narrow ledge of the unfinished windowsill. The sides of the shirt fell down her arms as she lifted herself up, gripping his broad shoulders for support.

"Over there," she said, darting a glance at the stairs.

Gaius slowed his strokes and grunted in question.

"Carry me to the stairs. I want . . . more." He pushed deep into her and she gasped, rolled her head back, and then shot another blazing look at him. "Please, Gaius."

He wrapped his arms around her backside and hoisted her up, his thick cock still solidly buried inside her. His big chest bunched under the strain of holding her weight, though he made no complaints as he carried them toward the stairwell. Setting one foot on the bottom step, he'd just begun to tilt her down when she pushed at his shoulder.

"No. You first," she said.

Gaius' brows twitched and his lips curled up. "Should've guessed you'd be bossy in bed too."

She clenched her core tight around his cock and he shuddered. "I'm not bossy just because I know how to ask for what I want."

With a low, rumbling laugh, he turned. Gripping the banister, he slowly lowered himself down to the unfinished wood step. Nessa's knees met the hard surface and the roughness bit into her skin, but she had the angle and leverage she needed now.

She leaned into him and he fell back to recline along the steps, returning his hands to her hips. His knees came up behind her as he set his feet one step higher to get the leverage to fuck into her. Nessa reached to brace her hands on the step his head rested on and lifted her hips, sliding off his deliciously thick length and back down, meeting his thrusts with urgent undulations of her hips.

The angle at which she braced herself above him placed her chest right at eye-level and he hungrily devoured her nipples, cupping and squeezing her breasts with both hands while his cock continued to slam up into her. Every stroke sent waves of pure pleasure through her body that were only amplified by his mouth on her breasts.

The angle was perfect in so many ways, the depth of his thrusts driving her to the brink in a way she'd never felt in her life. He was so big, so perfect, and the pleasure he gave her utterly divine. She'd often had her desserts described as "better than sex," but god, *nothing* she cooked had ever been better than *this*.

Pure pleasure pooled in her lower extremities, perfect little vibrations of ecstasy that increased in intensity with every deep stroke of Gaius' cock. His tempo increased, thrusts became harder, deeper, and Nessa's grasp on reality escaped her.

He tilted his head back and let out a roar when his orgasm took him. The hot flood of his seed blasted her core. She was so close, but too breathless to ask for what she needed.

Gaius kept pushing into her, his eyes clear and bright as he looked up at her. She was too lost with need, chasing the pleasure that hovered just at the edge of her grasp.

"You need more, baby?" he said, resting one hand on her hip as he slipped the other between them and found her throbbing clit.

"Yes, please!" she begged when he began to stroke her,

his cock still hard and filling her with excruciating pleasure. Gaius slid his other hand up to her head and pulled her down, grazing his lips across hers as he drove her to the brink with his steady fucking and perfect circular strokes over her clit.

"Come for me, Ness. That's right, baby. Let go."

Then he kissed her, the soft cushion of his beard tickling her skin as his tongue plunged between her lips, and she lost it. Her entire body shot through with wild, electric ecstasy and she slammed down onto his cock, arching her back as the sharp jolts rocketed through her.

Gaius kept his hand at the back of her neck, gripping her tightly. His gaze was fixed on her face, intent and every bit as hungry as it had been the entire time.

"Fuck, you're beautiful when you come," he said, grazing his thumb over her cheekbone when her tremors ebbed and she could focus on him again.

Nessa laughed. "You're pretty fucking epic. I think you probably scared off half the wildlife with that roar."

Her body felt languid and boneless, and she sank against Gaius' chest with a satisfied exhale. Her core still pulsed slightly around him, and she realized he was still fully hard.

With a little tilt of his hips, her desire surged again. He let out a groan as he gripped her ass and squeezed, holding her tight against him while he pushed deep into her.

His mouth grazed the edge of her ear. "Fuck, Ness. What are you doing to me?"

She pulled back to look down at him and lifted a shoulder. "Inspiring you, I hope?"

Gaius rumbled a half-laugh, half-growl and slipped his arm up her back. She abruptly found herself flipped and pinned against the hard ridges of the steps, her hips uncomfortably sandwiched between his groin and a sharp edge. But when he pulled back and slammed into her, she forgot everything but the pleasure of his cock buried deep inside her.

He gripped her by the knees and leaned back, his own knees resting on a lower step. When her legs splayed, he grabbed her hips and yanked her hard against him, her head bumping down onto the next step.

"Think you need a bed," she said, laughing when the stars stopped spinning and the pleasure started growing in her core again.

But he soon had her gasping again and crying his name, begging for him to fuck her harder. This time he slipped his hand between them early, rubbing her clit in tandem with the heavy, quick, thrusts of his cock. He drove her to the brink and stopped as if he knew exactly how close she was. Then he bent low, bracing his elbow on the step her shoulders rested on. The shift in angle pushed the tip of his cock harder against her sensitive inner wall and she gasped, pushing up into him and practically begging for him to make her come.

"Together, baby. This time, I'm waiting for you.

He pulled back out and pistoned into her, rubbing her clit harder. She clung to his back, nails digging in, her head tipped back as the unbearable ache grew to a peak and exploded within her.

"Gaius!" she cried, gripping him to her for dear life.

"Ness, fuck!" he yelled as he thrust into her once more, his cock swelling and erupting in a second flood of hot semen.

Gradually, the pleasure waned. He remained half-kneeling, hunched over her so he didn't crush her with his mouth pressed against her shoulder. His cock had softened, but as she started to move out from under him, he slipped his arm around her and held her, pushing deep once more, and once more spectacularly hard.

"My god, you're not seriously ready to go again?" she asked, staring up at him in astonishment.

"It's been a while, and you feel really fucking good."

"You know what doesn't feel good? Having my spine cut in half by these steps. Can we try a different spot now? Perhaps with a pillow?"

Gaius pushed into her once more, settling so deep she thought she could feel every single inch of his thick length, and it lit her up again like wildfire. But she was just as relieved as she was bereft when he slipped out and stood up. He gave her a long, hungry look before walking off, grumbling something about bossy women being the death of him.

CHAPTER TWELVE

NESSA

Nessa slowly rose, slipping the shirt back up her shoulders and resting her elbows on her knees. She let out a shaky breath and propped her chin on her hands, staring back out at the view. The ache of longing she'd had when she first saw the sunset had grown to a shamefully strong bout of pure envy. But buried deeper in her desire to have this place was the burning fire Gaius had ignited with that first kiss.

There wasn't much to the house itself, beyond her unshakable vision of what it could be if he found his inspiration again. But there was so much more to him than she'd realized. Even though he had a stubborn streak almost as wide as her own, she couldn't help but feel like she'd found her home.

And she didn't mean the place where her parents lived, or where she'd grown up. Her parents' house would always be home to her.

This was different, this bone-deep conviction that she was exactly where she belonged, and the very idea of leaving it, even to go back to her kitchen at Ig's and the little cottage in the garden, made her unreasonably sad.

Homesick. Which was a ridiculous thing to feel for a half-built house she'd only just set foot in that afternoon.

When Gaius stomped back in with a big bundle in his arms, her pulse quickened and she forced herself to shake off that feeling. Whatever this was, it was temporary, so she may as well enjoy it while she could. Perhaps they could at least stay friends once they got this out of their systems.

Because one thing she was sure of was that she wasn't finished with that big bear's body yet. Sweet fuck, the man was majestic, and he certainly had the stamina of a Champion despite his old injuries.

Gaius unfastened a buckled closure on the thick roll he held in his arms and flipped it out in the center of the big room. The moon was higher now and cast his shoulders in silvery light, enhancing the way his tattoo-adorned muscles bunched and rippled while he completed his task.

A hiss slithered out of the object he'd laid on the floor, and he stepped back as it expanded into a thick, narrow rectangle. He stooped down once and poked at a glowing button in the center of a little pad at the foot of the mattress, and it suddenly sprouted wings that flipped out and then lay flat as they inflated.

Nessa sat transfixed by him, even though all he did was stand there waiting for the bed to build itself. The man was all muscle, and lots of it. She would have loved to have seen him compete, but over the past week, she'd had ample opportunity to see him in action. He wielded his tools with perfect skill, so she could easily imagine him in the arena. Except when she witnessed him work, he was dressed in jeans and a t-shirt, which he wore exceptionally well, and focused his attacks on expertly cut lengths of lumber with a hammer and nails.

But he certainly hadn't worn those clothes better than he wore his own skin.

Nessa hopped off the steps and walked over to him, slipping up behind him to wrap her arms around his torso. He tensed for a second, then relaxed, a low, contented rumble vibrating through him as she pressed her breasts against his back and lay her cheek between his shoulder blades. He slipped the fingers of one hand through hers and raised it to his mouth, kissing the center of her palm. It was a tender gesture that made her heart beat faster and was completely at odds with the wild fucking they'd been doing moments ago.

He'd been ready to go again, but now Nessa was conflicted. Some part of her wanted nothing more than to just stay like this, with her skin flush against his and their breaths coming in tandem. The silent intimacy she shared with this man she'd barely gotten to know filled a hole in her she hadn't even known existed until tonight, and she dreaded the moment it would inevitably end.

Gaius turned in her arms and gazed down at her, the look in his eyes telling her he felt the same—that the moment was more precious than either of them were prepared for, and that neither of them were in a hurry to let it end.

Bending his head, he captured her mouth, sealing that silent communication with a confirmation that it didn't have to end yet. His hands drifted down her back and slipped up beneath the hem of her shirt to squeeze her ass and caress it. Nessa tilted her hips into his and found he'd roused to full hardness once more.

With a wicked tilt to her mouth, she pressed a hand

against his shoulder and pushed. Gaius fell onto his ass, landing on the bed in a patch of bright moonlight and gazing up at her with a fierce, defiant look.

Nessa half-expected him to complain again about how *bossy* she was, but instead he just reached for her, a low growl erupting from his throat. He yanked her to him, and she had no choice but to spread her thighs and straddle him or else bang into his bandaged knees. Her thighs slid against his hips and her soaked core grazed his hard length.

Any semblance of tenderness he'd displayed a moment ago was long gone. He urgently pushed the shirt off her shoulders, tearing it away impatiently.

"Thought you wanted me in that thing," she said, laughing.

"Need you naked more." He pushed his hips up into hers, making her gasp at the raw, silken heat of his cock as it grazed her tender folds. His big hands roamed up and down her back, his beard brushing against her chest as he covered her neck in kisses and soft bites, gradually moving down to pepper her breasts with more.

All the while he tortured her with the slow, languid thrusts of his hips, rubbing the length of his shaft along the slick, swollen flesh between her thighs to the point she was close to climax again.

She tried pushing him back so she could climb on and fuck him, but he just growled and gripped her ass harder, grinding his hips more fervently against hers.

"Dammit! I need you inside me so bad."

"How bad?" he asked.

"Gaius, will you just lay down so I can fuck you?"

He chuckled around her nipple and lifted his eyes as his lips popped off the tip of her breast. "How bad do you need it, Ness? I think maybe it's not bossy if you beg."

It was her turn to growl. "Down," she said, pushing with bear strength against both shoulders this time. Gaius went, laughing up at the moon as she moved to straddle his cock.

"Hang on, baby," he said. "Let's do this right." He hooked an arm around her and pushed himself farther up the bed until they were fully on it, bathed in moonlight. "Better?"

"Yes. Much." She braced her hands on his chest and fixed her gaze on his as she lifted her hips again and positioned him between her thighs. His tip pierced her perfectly, sliding deep with a long, smooth stroke that she savored every second of. She dropped her head back as she began to move, enraptured by the sensation of his entire length receding from her before plunging back in hard.

They maintained a slower tempo than before, Gaius seeming content to let her set the pace. When she glanced down at him, he had both hands propped under his head as though he were merely a spectator to their fucking. He seemed entertained more than involved, which irritated her.

"What are you doing?" she asked.

"Getting fucked by a gorgeous she-bear. You wanted to be on top, baby. I want to lay back and watch you take care of yourself on my cock. Make yourself come on me."

She lifted off him and sank back down, slower now, enjoying the way his gaze heated with each slow increment of her sheath encompassing his length.

"I don't need you to get myself off," she said. "I could just go home and finish."

"But you won't. You're enjoying yourself way too much, and so am I. So let's compromise. You got me on my back, now let me boss you around a little. Make yourself come, baby."

The slow strokes along his length were affecting her sanity. She desperately wanted to come, but after the last two rounds had somehow built up an expectation that he would be the one to do it.

"I want you to come with me," she said, though the excuse was a weak objection.

"Honey, I'm ready to explode right now. Just waiting for the right moment to let go. Now touch yourself."

Her thighs ached from the slow lift and fall of her hips against his, and she almost wished for him to flip her over again and nail her hard like he had before. But she did as he demanded anyway, the bossy bastard.

Sliding her fingers between her thighs, she found her clit, slick and hot and unbelievably swollen with need. She couldn't help but gasp as she gave herself one light stroke, her eyelids fluttering closed at the intensity. Her channel clenched hard around him and he emitted a low growl of encouragement as he rose up to meet her downward thrusts.

Biting her lower lip, she couldn't help but watch his face as he watched her. She clutched one breast, squeezing and pinching her nipple while she swirled her fingers between her thighs in quicker strokes, a rush of sensation already flooding her lower extremities.

Gaius' lips parted and his chest heaved. His eyes blazed with need and he dropped his hands to her hips, squeezing and urging her to a quicker tempo.

He'd taken over control, easily guiding her up and down his cock as he rocked his own hips into her with increasingly needy, violent thrusts. Nessa's eyelids fluttered half-closed and she let out a long, rough moan when her orgasm blasted through her. Gaius looked completely enraptured at her crumbling, and a second later, he slammed hard into her and held her tight against his hips as his cock pulsed. The slow throbbing beat of him sent prolonged tremors through her body and she licked her lips, exhausted yet unwilling to move just yet and interrupt the delicious sensations.

His body relaxed by increments, his cock slowly softening inside her. He reached up and pulled her down to his chest, kissing her deeply and wrapping his strong arms around her torso. She settled against him, oddly content and more sated than she'd ever been after sex.

CHAPTER
THIRTEEN
NESSA

Nessa returned to semi-consciousness later. She must have dozed for a while, because the room was dark, the moon having moved across the sky and no longer bestowing its light on their little tryst. Gaius held her close, body curled around hers, his warm, hard chest pressed against her back. It had grown chilly, but she was toasty warm, thanks to the blankets he must have covered them with while she slept.

She felt so damn good she didn't want to leave, but spending the entire night in the man's bed would set a terrible precedent. They could only coexist professionally. The fact that they'd had mind-blowing sex for hours that night didn't change how they would have to act toward one another during the day.

Nessa eased herself out of his embrace, hoping the evening fog hadn't descended yet and soaked her clothes through yet again where they hung on his clothesline outside. She could sneak out, take the rest of the weekend to come to her senses, and shake this weird need she'd acquired since visiting him—the need to stay despite all indications that it was a bad idea.

She swallowed when she saw how far the edge of the bed was. Had the thing somehow gotten bigger while she slept? Slowly, she crawled toward the far end, practically holding her breath so she didn't wake him. She barely made it a couple feet when he reached out, gripped her wrist, and squeezed.

"Oh, no you don't," Gaius rumbled. He rose up and toppled her over, pressing her back into the bed as he straddled her.

"Gaius," she breathed. "I should go home. This was nice, but..."

"But what? You don't like my bed? If you want, we can move back to the stairs."

"Your bed's fine. I just need to go."

"For what? I know Ig and Bry are gone all weekend for the annual League banquet. You don't need to be anywhere but in my bed. You're staying."

Nessa bristled. "I don't need a *reason*. If I want to go, I'm going!"

Gaius shook his head and settled himself between her thighs. His elbows sank into the bed on either side of her and his face hovered just above hers, his breath tickling her lips. Nessa's heartbeat sped up when she realized he was hard again, his cock hot and heavy against her hip.

"The thing is, I don't believe you really want to go, do you?" He drifted his lips across her cheek from the corner of her mouth to the sensitive skin beneath her ear. His beard tickled in the most delicious way, sending a tingling rush of sensation to her nipples and straight between her thighs. "You wouldn't have even gotten into my bed to begin with, if you didn't want to be here."

"Gaius, we need to be adults about this. The sex was great, but it's a bad idea to get comfortable."

His mouth and tongue tickled over her shoulder as he slipped lower, one big hand palming her breast before he tweaked her nipple, making her gasp. "Like I said, the stairs are right over there. But you're not going home until I'm done with you."

Nessa groaned, partly from frustration and partly from the delicious pleasure that flooded her when he captured her nipple between his lips and sucked hard. She involuntarily lifted her hips, aching for more contact between her thighs. Her entire body craved more of him. It was crazy she could want more after the night they'd already had, but she did.

"You are infuriating," she complained, but didn't move when he slid down and knelt between her thighs. He slipped his hands down over her sides, beneath her legs, and pushed them wide. There was no mistaking his intention, and her core flooded with want for exactly what his gaze promised.

Gaius licked his lips as he parted her folds with his thumbs, sliding one digit through the flooded channel before sinking it into her.

"Pretty sure all this has nothing to do with the idea of climbing into your own bed alone."

"Please..."

"Please what? I know you want to tell me, Ness. You want my dick, or my tongue? Your choice."

He slipped his thumb back out of her and began rubbing slow, tight circles over her clit.

Her body buzzed with need and she tilted her hips up into his touch. Then he stopped.

She glared at him.

"You're the boss here, baby. What do you want?"

Her bear was already beside itself, ready to pounce on him. He had asked for a decision. Either-or. But she wanted it all.

"Your tongue," she finally said. "Lick me. Make me come with your mouth. *Then* I want you to fuck me, but . . ." The image of what she craved—what her she-bear growled for—flitted through her mind.

"But?" Gaius prompted.

"When you fuck me, do it from behind."

He bared his teeth in a salacious grin. "You got it, babe."

He immediately settled against the mattress, pushing her knees up so his broad shoulders pressed against her backside with his palms holding her spread open as far as she could go. Beginning with a slow lick, he traced her cleft with the tip of his tongue all the way from her ass to her clit, drawing out the action until she groaned. He seemed intent on teasing her, probably because he wanted to make her beg again, but she wouldn't give him the satisfaction.

He tortured her for several more minutes with long, slow licks, each one greater proof of how fucking amazing he was at using that tongue. Nessa began to mentally plot her revenge, and the very idea of having her mouth on his cock drove her need to greater heights.

Finally she lost patience and tangled her fingers in his hair, forcing his mouth over her clit. "Suck, damn you. Use your tongue there, on my clit."

His shoulders shook and a low, amused rumble rolled from him, sending pleasant waves of vibration through his mouth and straight into her core.

"My pleasure," he murmured against her flesh. A second later, he assaulted her aching clit with the perfect combination of sucking and licking, so quick and relentless she completely lost track of all sensation except what she felt between her thighs. Within moments, he had her at the edge and flying over with a loud yell, yanking at his hair and bucking up into his mouth.

Before she'd even had a chance to come down, he grabbed her hips with both hands and flipped her over. He dragged her hips up off the bed and slammed his cock into her soaked pussy so hard she let out a yelp of surprise.

Gaius' rough grunts and rutting thrusts had her soaring again within seconds, and when he slid a thumb between her ass cheeks and pressed into her tight hole, she lost her mind completely. Her body clenched around him with her most mind-blowing climax yet, her cries this time coming out as hitching, gasping sobs that sounded completely unlike her. But he sounded less than himself as well, his voice rising in a roar that might have shattered glass if his house had windows.

He hunched over her as his cock pulsed into her, teeth grazing her shoulder and leaving a tingling sensation and a weird longing behind. It was as if he'd thought to mark her, but decided against it, and she was both grateful and strangely disappointed.

He hooked his arm around her waist and held her tight as he rolled them onto their sides, his cock still solidly buried deep in her. She reached for the blanket and tugged it partway up her body, Gaius grabbing the edge and covering them both as he settled against her with a low rumble of contentment.

"You're staying," he said again, as if the argument hadn't already been settled when he promised her oral sex.

Nessa smiled to herself and bit her lip as she clenched her core around his half-hard shaft. "I'm a little trapped, so I guess I have no choice."

Gaius let out a low noise of approval, pushed his hips into her, and then relaxed.

Nessa let go of the worry as well as she could. The truth was that she really *didn't* want to leave. But that was the problem.

The next time she woke up, the room was awash in a dim glow and Gaius' calloused hands were sliding over her body in slow caresses, squeezing and touching every inch of her he could reach. Heavy thickness stretched her core, the delicious fullness of his cock instantly heating her blood once again. How the hell could she still long to be fucked? She'd never been such a crazed, wanton woman in her life.

But good god, she still wanted him.

She let out a moan of pleasure and pushed back into him, enjoying the languid rocking of his hips into hers from behind. He kept up the rough caresses, his mouth pressed to her ear and his panting breaths gusting hot across her cheek.

"Can't fucking get enough of you, Ness. Fuck, what you do to me..."

"Don't stop," she said, even though he had shown no signs of ever stopping. He slipped a hand down her leg and gripped her knee, lifting her leg high to give himself better access. Behind her, he shifted positions, adjusting his legs and lifting his hips to spear her more directly.

Nessa twisted her torso so she could see him. At that moment, one of Astreia's two suns broke over the mountains outside and gilded Gaius' body in a beautiful glow. Instead of silver, all the gray threads in his hair and beard turned gold. His intricate tattoos stood out against his lighter skin now backlit by the sunrise.

Nessa's breath escaped her at the glorious sight, with his curly mop of dark hair shot through with the light half-hanging over his bearded face, his blue eyes intense as he slowly fucked her. He looked weary, yet for all the world, still intent on her pleasure. His cock thickened inside her and he shuddered, his mouth falling partway open. Without any cue from her, he slipped his hand down her thigh and found her clit, rubbing it in the perfect rhythmic tempo to drive her to the brink with him.

They came in a tangle of limbs, Gaius wrapping his arms around her as he continued thrusting into her. At the very moment of their shared orgasm, the second sun burst over the horizon, flooding the entire house in brilliant light.

Gaius landed on his side in front of her, their legs still entwined. He gave her a semi-irritated look belied by the twitching pull of a smile at the corner of his mouth. "I'm too damn old for this."

Nessa giggled. "Don't blame me. If you'd let me leave last night, you could've gotten more sleep."

As if roused by the sunrise, both their bellies rumbled in unison. They gave each other equal looks of shock, then burst into laughter. When their mirth subsided, Nessa said, "I saw breakfast fixings in your fridge out there. I'll go get something started."

She started to slip out of bed, hunting around for his old shirt as she made her way to the edge.

"Not a chance," Gaius said, easily climbing out of bed and ambling naked toward the door to the deck. "My house. My kitchen. I cook."

Nessa stared after him, filled with both envy and disappointment. She had yet to have him eat a meal of hers, but she couldn't very well bully him out of his own kitchen to prove herself. With a little huff, she snatched up the shirt off the floor and tossed it on, following him out the door.

It was hard to sulk for long. She sat by the dormant fire pit and propped her elbows on her knees, opting to enjoy the view of a big, naked, and perfectly proportioned bear cooking for her.

"I could get used to this," she said in a warning tone.

Gaius chuffed and glanced at her as he whipped up whatever passed for breakfast to him. Then he came over and stoked up the banked coals until a low fire burned in the pit.

"Better get comfortable, Ness, because I plan to make sure you get used to it."

CHAPTER
FOURTEEN
GAIUS

Gaius wasn't sure exactly when he'd decided he had to have her as his mate. For all he knew, the desire could have been building since they first set eyes on each other, or when he'd first seen her naked. Possibly it was when she'd tended to his aching knees with such no-nonsense, yet tender care. Or maybe it was during the fifth or sixth time he made her come that first night and still craved more.

Probably it was when he'd first seen her wearing his old shirt.

Whenever it was didn't matter, because despite spending an entire weekend either making love in his bed, under the waterfall, or around his unfinished house, he could tell she was holding something back. When he was inside her, she was all his, giving herself to him whole-heartedly. But when they took a break to eat or, god forbid, *sleep*, he sensed her distance herself from him bit by bit.

The end of the weekend came far too soon for his satisfaction. She'd been either naked or in his old shirt for two days straight, but when she slipped her own clothes back on, it was like a wall went up. She was still chipper and as bossy as ever, giving him final instructions on the liniment recipe for his knees. The only difference was that the bossiness made him want to take her back to bed just to hear her beg.

But he restrained himself, settling into quiet contemplation after her transporter disappeared down his driveway. He wasn't sure how to break through that resistance, even though he was damn sure they were meant for each other.

Shaking his head, he wandered back into his house, deciding to take advantage of the remaining afternoon light to scratch a different itch.

He threw off the tarp that covered his building materials still stacked in the middle of the empty house. He'd need to order more soon, but he had enough to get started on the bedroom. He was damn sure going to have her in his bed again, but the next time she came, he wanted a proper bed to make love to her in.

CHAPTER
FIFTEEN
NESSA

Nessa hesitated on her way out the door of the garden cottage. She was already late getting breakfast started for Ig and Bry, who would be finishing their dawn training and starving before too long. But for some inconceivable reason, Gaius had decided to show up early that morning, and the sounds of power tools and hammering had thrown her off.

She wasn't ready to see him again. What the hell had she been thinking, spending the entire weekend with him? She'd probably given him entirely the wrong idea. And now she'd have to face him and deal with the consequences—the inevitable cold, growly dismissal.

Bracing herself, she let out a sigh and pushed through the doors, stalked across the garden, and in through the open door to the construction zone that would soon be her kitchen in Ig's big house. It wasn't until she stepped in that it occurred to her she could've easily walked around the house the long way to get to the lower level.

But it was too late. Gaius saw her and immediately

turned off the saw. "Morning, Ness," he said with a smile and a wave.

"Hi! Morning!" she chirped. "I'm late, gotta go." She hurried past him without a glance back. If she didn't hang around, she wouldn't have the opportunity to say something dumb that would set him off and make him stop liking her.

After breakfast, she sat with her meal planning notebooks, struggling to focus. The damn dumbwaiter carried every single sound down from the new kitchen, and along with the rhythmic sound of Gaius hammering, she couldn't help but picture his muscles flexing. At first it was just the image of him wielding his hammer like the pro he was, but eventually the image of him above her, pounding into her with rhythmic precision, was the thing that got stuck in her head.

"Hey, Ness. Ready to go tear out some vines?" Levi said, popping his head through her door.

"God, yes." Nessa hopped up and followed him out the door. At least Levi's constant chatter would distract her from thoughts of the big bear.

She managed to avoid seeing Gaius for the rest of the day. The hammering sounds stopped around mid-afternoon, signaling that he'd probably finished for the day and gone home. She went about the rest of the evening meal prep in a better frame of mind, now that the distraction of his work wasn't bombarding her.

She accepted Ig's invitation to sit with him and Bry for supper and entertained herself listening to their banter about the recent banquet and their various conquests. Ig was ahead this year on their annual bet to see who'd bed the most female fans during the off-season. She felt sorry for the pair—when they finally met their actual mates, their dragons would have nothing to do with the bet anymore.

Still, they were two of her closest friends, and sharing a bottle of wine and chatting with them made her feel somewhat normal, and at least *sane* again. There was no harm in enjoying a weekend of fun with Gaius, so she just needed to get over her sense that she'd left something unfinished with him.

It was probably just a side-effect of all that amazing sex. She wanted more, but she'd survive without it. The man wanted something different, or else the matchmaker Oracle would probably have matched them up already. Celestial Soul Mates had both their details, and had for some time.

"You're looking unusually broody tonight, Nessa," Ig said, pulling her out of her reverie. "Is the kitchen not coming out the way you'd hoped?"

"What? Oh, no. The kitchen's fine. Gaius is . . ." She sighed. "He's fine."

Ig and Bry exchanged a glance, then Ig said. "I didn't actually ask about Gaius, but that's good to hear. He seemed more energized than usual this morning when he started. Guess retirement's starting to agree with him."

Bryer chuckled and took a swallow of his wine. "That's good. Maybe the old grouch will finally finish that house of his. He ought to get it done if he's hoping to bring a mate home soon."

Nessa frowned and shook her head. "No. I think he's right to wait. I mean, he should want to build a place his mate would want to live in, right? How's he going to know what that is without knowing who *she* is first?"

Ig sat back with an indulgent smile. "You don't think I plan on remodeling this place whenever I find a mate, do you?"

Nessa scoffed. "You two aren't even close to retiring. By the time you do, the place will probably be due for a remodel. Which is fine, as long as you keep the kitchen, because I plan on using it for a long, long time."

"Or he finds the perfect mate-slash-chef by then," Bryer said. "Besides, doesn't your mom have the matchmaker hooking you up with a clan leader the very second there's one worth snagging? I swear, every time I see Mrs. Baxter, she goes on about something that Oracle told her. It all sounds like mystical bullshit to me. After all the women we've been with, you've got to think our odds of finding our mates are getting bigger—the pool to choose from definitely isn't growing. I don't think that matchmaker has anything special going on that we can't tap into ourselves."

"I'm with you," Nessa said. "If I was meant to be with *any* of the eligible heirs out there, they'd have hooked us up by now. Maybe we are all lost causes."

Ig and Bry laughed and toasted to being lost causes. Nessa went along with it, but her chest hurt at the reminder of her conversation with Gaius that weekend. He was an amazing, talented, caring man. There was no way in hell there couldn't be a mate out there for him. No doubt the matchmaker Oracle would call soon, and Nessa wanted to make sure she was well out of the picture by then, because she didn't think she could handle it when it happened.

She let Ig's housekeeper, Ren, finish cleaning up after supper and said goodbye to her friends. Out of habit, she wandered up the interior staircase from the kitchen to the first floor, still buzzed from the wine and itching to see today's progress on the kitchen.

The scent of fresh paint hit her nostrils as she exited the stairwell, and she stopped short when she encountered a wall that hadn't existed that morning. The kitchen was now blocked off from the rest of the house, the wall and swinging doors in place, and the wiring for light fixtures in what would become the dining room dangling from the high ceiling.

She pushed through the doors and was instantly awash in a cascade of comforting colored lights. It was sunset, and though the kitchen faced east, the lights were designed to mimic the changing tones of the sky at the different times of day.

She marveled at the interior. The counters and cabinets were finished and painted, the tile floors installed and cleaned. Gaius' tools were still strewn about, and there were a few obvious areas that weren't finished yet, the dumbwaiter being one of them. It still sat mockingly in the wall, clearly untouched and waiting for her to give Gaius the go-ahead. For whatever reason, he'd neglected to cover it back up, and she guiltily recalled her insistence that he allow her to cook for him as a remedy for his old arena injuries.

She should just get over her reticence to see him. They'd had one fun weekend. And what of it? They were adults, and should be able to behave like adults around each other despite that past, because it was exactly that: *past*. She'd probably never forget it, but it was ridiculous to dwell on it.

She trailed her hand across the smooth, marble countertop that stretched along one wall. The choice of materials was deliberate, and exactly to her specifications. She had solid wood chopping block counters in one area, stainless steel in another, and marble here, all to serve different culinary purposes.

Wandering around the corner, Nessa found the door to what she knew was the new pantry and opened it. She let out a gasp when she found the interior completely finished with rows upon rows of shelves outfitted with rolling rails.

The door to the cooler was set into one wall. The cooler hadn't even been there that morning—how the hell had she missed the big contraption being delivered?

The rest of the equipment had yet to arrive, but with this installed, she could start planning more long-term meals and canning summer fruits and vegetables.

She stepped back out of the cooler and shut it behind her, beyond thrilled at the amount of work that had been completed in a single day.

"You like?" a deep voice said, making her jump.

Gaius stood in the pantry doorway, leaning against the frame. He looked like he'd just showered, and even smelled like the woody-scented soap he kept on a little stone ledge by his waterfall.

"Hi . . . I thought you'd gone home for the day."

"I did, but there was something I forgot to finish."

Nessa laughed. "Are you kidding? You did so much, all in one day! You've more than earned a break."

"That may be," Gaius said. "But this is something that would keep me up if I didn't come back down here and take care of it."

His gaze raked over her with a lazy heat that left her entire body warm in its wake. Her breath caught in her throat when he took a step toward her, and she instinctively backed up, only to find her backside flush against the inset counter along the pantry's back wall.

"Oh? W-What is it? You need my help?"

"I do." With a slow nod, he closed in on her in a few more steps, crowding into her space, his sweet, clean aroma inundating her senses and sending a flood of warmth into her core. He braced both hands against the edge of the counter behind her, caging her in. "This is something that absolutely cannot be done without you, in fact."

He leaned down and brushed his lips along her temple, breathing in deeply as though inhaling her scent into his lungs. Nessa let out a shuddering sigh at that brief contact and reflexively pressed her hands to his chest, though she wasn't sure if she wanted to push him away or drag him close.

"You smell so damn delicious. I can't help but remember a little promise you made me the other night..."

"I know. I'll have a menu prepped for you tomorrow. You'll love it, I promise."

He let out a growl that came from deep in his chest as his lips trailed down her cheek and settled against her jaw just beneath her ear. "The thing is, I think you're my cure, Ness. I felt no pain today, and the only thing that changed was having you in my bed for two nights in a row."

She shook her head and pushed back against him. "It was the liniment, that's all," she breathed, finding it hard to fill her lungs with his big body monopolizing all the air in the room. She needed room to breathe, to think... because this want he filled her with was only a recipe for heartbreak when the matchmaker Oracle found him a real mate.

"I'd rather not chance it." His lips grazed the side of her throat as he dropped one hand to her hip and squeezed, pulling her tight against him. The air left Nessa's lungs in a sharp exhale at the rigid length of him that pressed against her lower abdomen. Every single memory of everything he'd made her feel over the weekend rushed back, as though she hadn't already been dwelling on it all day long.

"No, you better not chance it," she said.

His lips traced the line of her jaw and paused at the

corner of her mouth. "So, you're the boss here, Ness. What's your recipe to keep the pain away?"

Her need for caution and distance disappeared with his subtle taunt. He wanted to tease her, but she would have none of it.

"Just kiss me, damnit."

Gaius pulled back and laughed. "There she is," he said, looking down at her with a wicked glint in his eyes. "Missed you, bossy girl..."

"Oh, for fuck's sake..." She hooked her hand at the back of his neck and yanked him down, their mouths crashing together in a sweet, rough tangle of lips and tongues. Gaius' low chuckle transformed into a groan that resonated deep in her belly. Her entire body felt heavy and swollen with need to have his hands on her, his cock inside her. She broke away from the kiss long enough to tell him as much.

"I need you inside me *now*," she commanded, tearing his shirt off over his head. She raked her nails down through the dark curls that covered his tattooed chest and was gratified when he tore at the opening of her wrap-around dress until her breasts sprang free. His mouth went to her nipples as he hoisted her up with both hands and set her on the countertop behind her. They tore at each other's clothes, his hands up her skirt, yanking down her panties, her hands at his belt, tugging it free and unfastening his pants.

Mere seconds after she had his cock free, he'd hauled her to the edge of the counter and buried himself inside her. They let out synchronous moans of pleasure, and Nessa's entire body from the tips of her toes all the way into the depths of her connection with her bear rejoiced at the fullness of their joining. This was what she needed. Oh god, how could she ever stop wanting this?

Gaius was more intense and single-minded than the first time they'd made love, driving into her with a kind of fury Nessa had never witnessed before. It was as though he were claiming her body, and her bear responded with a roar of acceptance. She surrendered to his touch because it felt too good not to, yet when he grazed his teeth over her shoulder, she pulled away, digging her heels into his ass and her nails into his back. The distraction worked—his head flew back and he let out a roar as he climaxed.

Nessa's chest heaved, her body still alight from the pleasure left unspent. But Gaius only paused for a second before slipping out of her and falling to his knees, his jeans still bunched around his hips. He pushed her thighs wide, holding them up while he buried his mouth against her soaked folds.

"Gaius! Oh god, yes!" She tangled the fingers of one hand into his hair and braced herself on her other hand as he tongued her to oblivion. She'd been close already, but the intense flicks of his tongue against her needy clit sent her hurtling over the edge almost instantaneously.

She sat gasping for breath as he rose and swiped a hand over his beard. "Come home with me, Ness. We can do this all night."

Her bear let out an interested little rumble, but Nessa nixed it. "We have an early start. We should get some rest," she said, even though nothing sounded more divine than falling asleep to the moonrise, wrapped up in Gaius' big arms.

Gaius regarded her in silence for a moment, his expression still filled with hunger, though she sensed it was for something more than her body... definitely more than she was willing to give. Finally he stepped close again and cradled her head in his hand. He leaned down to eye-level, his face close to hers.

"I will have you in my bed again, Ness. That's a promise. It doesn't have to be tonight, but it's happening."

Nessa swallowed and gave him what she hoped passed for a flirty smile, though it belied the tangled knots in her belly. "We'll see," she said, then she kissed him to break the intensity of the look he gave her.

After he left, she let out a long breath and readjusted her dress. She retreated to her cottage and climbed into bed, curling into a ball to try to banish the ache in her belly. She wanted so much to give in to his request, but she couldn't go back there. The two nights she'd spent had been two nights too many.

It was crazy; the house was nothing more than an empty shell. There wasn't much to be excited about. But she wanted the life it represented so badly she could taste it.

She wanted *him*, but he wasn't meant to be hers. If he was, the Oracle would have told her so already.

CHAPTER
SIXTEEN
GAIUS

Gaius climbed the stairs to the second floor of his house and stood in the center of the room, remembering that first sight of Nessa in his old shirt with the backdrop of the sunset behind her. He'd probably done this all wrong, not finishing the house *before* having a woman here, but Nessa hadn't exactly given him a choice. She had just blown in like a force of nature, insinuating herself in his life to such a degree he could no longer picture anything but her vision of this house, right along with her curvy body living here with him.

He watched the vista beyond the railing for several minutes, trying to work out some kind of strategy for convincing her to return—and making her stay. Something had obviously spooked her, though he couldn't imagine what. She had clearly loved this place, so much so that she'd reminded him of all the reasons *he* loved it. And that had inspired him to finish it.

He'd begun yesterday afternoon, immediately after she left, and the product of his work rested in the center of the room now. The bed he'd built lacked only a finish, but the naked wood had its own stark beauty. It was enough to sleep on for now.

Gaius ran his hand over the smoothly sanded footboard and up the hand-carved post. He should sleep. He was exhausted after spending half the night building the thing. Yet he couldn't bring himself to climb in it alone, and he was at a loss as to how to entice her to join him again.

Instead he left the big bed behind, returning to his hammock out on the back deck near the waterfall.

He would get her to come back one way or the other, even if he had to finish the whole damn house before it happened.

CHAPTER
SEVENTEEN
GAIUS

Early the next morning, Gaius eyeballed the renovation plans with Ignazio, working out a schedule for demolition of the old kitchen that would avoid upsetting Nessa's schedule. The dumbwaiter cranked into gear with a low hum, and Ignazio glanced at the door to the contraption and back to Gaius.

"You expecting something?" Ignazio asked.

"Could be . . . Nessa insisted on feeding me to see if it'd help with the pain in my knees. I guess she's following through."

When the dumbwaiter motor stopped, he ambled over and slid the door open. Inside rested a huge tray with several covered dishes. A little note read, *"This is half the remedy. See me for the other half."*

He smiled to himself as he carried the tray over to the kitchen island and pulled up a stool. Ig leaned across the island, inhaling deeply. "Damn, that smells even better than what she usually serves us for breakfast. I hope this means we're getting something special today."

As Gaius started lifting lids, his belly rumbled, and his

bear emitted a hungry growl in harmony. Nessa had sent up a plate filled with an omelet overloaded with vegetables, a side of smoked fish, and a bowl of hot cereal with fresh berries. Accompanying it was a carafe of freshly squeezed juice.

"The other half . . . What's this?" Ig asked, holding up the note.

Gaius popped a piece of the fish into his mouth and savored it, answering Ig with a noncommittal grunt. "More herbal remedy shit, I guess," he said, shifting his focus back to the food as he dug in, the demolition plans entirely forgotten.

Ig set the note down and leaned his elbows on the kitchen island across from Gaius. "Really?" he said with a skeptical note. "You sure she's not offering something more . . . hands-on?"

Gaius ignored the warmth creeping up his neck. He was positive what Nessa offered was precisely what Ig insinuated, but hell if he was going to share that with the other man. They'd been friends since Ig and Bry joined the League together, but he didn't pry into the boys' dumb bet, and he wasn't about to share intimate details of his own life with them.

Ignazio clenched his hands into fists, his knuckles cracking as he lifted a finger and pointed it in Gaius' face. "Blackpaw, whatever the fuck you're doing with my chef, she had better not get hurt, you got it? I will burn your shit down if I catch wind that she's been damaged in any way. And that isn't just my stomach talking. Ness is family."

Gaius set down his fork and finished chewing his food. He slowly lifted his gaze to Ignazio and looked the dragon squarely in his red eyes. "Not that it's any of your business, but Nessa's more than just some diversion to while away a summer between seasons. She is sustenance. The main fucking course, as opposed to an appetizer. The kind of woman who won't leave you craving anything once she's done with you."

Ignazio stood up straighter, looking a little abashed at the subtle dig, but the man had it coming. The Hot Wings bet had never been a secret and had earned them a reputation as players, but Gaius could see the dragon was maybe a little ashamed of it now.

Ignazio cleared his throat. "That's good to hear, as long as she feels the same way."

Gaius nodded. "She's being a little hardheaded about it, but I think she'll come around. Trust me . . . if she doesn't want what I have to offer, she'll say so."

A sharp laugh escaped Ig's mouth and he relaxed. "Yeah, Nessa's never been one to mince words. That's one thing I love about her—you always know right where you stand. Hopefully when Bry and I retire, we'll be able to find a woman half as together as she is. If she were the one, you can be damn sure I'd throw away the rules and mate her now."

"Good thing she's mine and not yours, you crazy bastard."

Ignazio sobered, his brows pulling together. "Shit, you really mean that, don't you? You two have known each other how long? A week?"

"Long enough for my bear to know. Just don't fucking say anything to her. It's between me and her, got it?"

"No worries, man. But didn't you meet with an matchmaker Oracle when you first retired?"

Gaius winced. It had been so long he'd almost forgotten. "Yeah, I need to get in touch with Ms. Delphine. Have her call off the search. I just want to be sure it's mutual."

Ig tapped on the note. "This is a good sign. She's never been one to get this close to a guy. Trust me, Bry and I watched her like hawks when she was growing up. She never did casual, so if she gets this close, she's got a damn good reason. If there's anything Bry or I can do to help, just say so."

Gaius nodded and dug back into his food as Ignazio headed for the door.

Looking back over his shoulder, Ignazio said, "I see why this room is likely to be the first one finished. Remind me to thank her once you guys figure things out."

Gaius took his time savoring the meal, then went back to work, pausing every half hour or so until he heard the telltale trumpeting of a pair of dragons pulling drills over the lake. He set the tray of empty dishes back into the dumbwaiter and sent it back down with a note to Nessa: *"Still hungry. Coming down for 2nd course."*

His cock was nearly at full mast when he pushed through the doors into the old kitchen. Immediately her scent washed over him, and he realized it wasn't just her—it was the entire kitchen. The room itself was infused with scents that reminded him of her, as though her presence filled the entire space. She had said she grew up in this kitchen, but it hadn't hit him until now how much it smelled like her. More so now, since she was currently here.

He stopped inside the door to catch his breath, his need skyrocketing so high he lost focus.

She came into view and his vision tunneled, his bear's instincts surging to the surface. His nostrils flared and his mouth watered at the sweet aroma of arousal he was already half-addicted to. She wore another dark, wrap-around dress like she'd had on the night before, only this one was dotted with white circles, reminding him of the full moon they'd made love beneath their first night together.

She said something, but he was too far gone to comprehend words. He swooped down and lifted her into his arms, devouring her mouth like she hadn't already fed him one of the best meals of his life.

Nessa didn't protest or complain. She simply let out an impatient noise and scrabbled at his shirt until she had it yanked off over his head again like the night before. She had his fly open and her hand in his pants, stroking him within a few more seconds, her urgent touch making him dizzy from the loss of blood flow to his head.

Somehow he found a chair and sat with Nessa astride him, and a second later, he was encompassed in her delicious, tight depths, her fingers digging into his shoulders as she rode him. He freed her breasts, infinitely grateful for Astreia ingenuity where women's clothing was concerned. It was like her dress had been designed with the needs of rutting mates in mind.

Nessa fucked him even more desperately than the night before, slipping her hand between her legs to toy with her clit. Gaius clutched her full, round ass in both hands, spreading her and guiding her hips up and down his cock while he devoured her nipples with teeth and tongue.

The clenching pull of her sheath tightened and she arched her back, yelling his name as her body quivered and tightened in release. Gaius let out a curse into the soft hollow between her breasts, his cock erupting into her with sudden, violent spurts.

She slowed and then stopped, her breathing rough against his ear. Resting her forehead on his shoulder, she hummed in satisfaction. He held her tighter to his chest, more than sated physically, but somehow regretful that this felt so much like a secret tryst, and that the two of them would go back to avoiding each other except for these furtive, stolen moments.

Gaius nuzzled at her cheek and she sighed, turning her head just enough for their mouths to meet. The kiss felt desperate, needy, and the accompanying tightness around his cock awoke his bear's hunger again. He twisted them both and rose, laying Nessa on the table beside them in one smooth movement as he spread her thighs and began to fuck into her again in earnest.

She did something to him; there was no denying it. The way he ended a round of fucking hungrier for her than when they started had to be abnormal, but he couldn't get enough of her, and she clearly suffered from the same problem.

He fucked her harder this time, now that he had control and the leverage to pound into her. She cried out in encouragement, as demanding as ever, and he loved it. He especially loved it when her hands went to her head and she arched her back. She cried out as her gorgeous breasts bounced from the rhythm of his thrusts, and he couldn't help but bend over and capture one dark nipple between his lips and suck hard. Her orgasm was harsher than before, and he climaxed immediately after with her heels digging in hard to his backside.

Curious how she'd respond this time, he pressed his lips to her shoulder and tentatively bared his teeth, raking his sharp incisors lightly over her skin just enough for her to feel them, but not enough to break skin. If he was going to mark her, he damn well wanted her fully on board.

But the way she jerked and pushed him up was a clear indication she wasn't ready, even though the feral look in her eyes spoke directly to his bear. Her *animal* wanted this, but for some reason, *she* was holding back.

He gave her space, accepting a clean kitchen towel to wipe up with as she turned away and put herself back together. Her long, dark hair was pulled back in a thick braid, tendrils of which had come free in the midst of their wild lovemaking. She was utterly gorgeous like this, still flushed, her lips swollen from his kiss and his scent all over her. She looked for all the world like she could go again—and she smelled like it too—yet she leaned back against the sink with her arms crossed, looking everywhere but at him while he fastened his pants and found his shirt.

A knock sounded at the door and they both jumped like they'd been shocked. Levi popped his head in. "Ness, ready for some more planting? We've got fruit trees!"

Gaius glared at the young cheetah shifter, whose eyes widened and mouth popped open in a prelude to an apology.

"I'll be right there, Levi," Nessa called to him before he could say anything.

Levi nodded and disappeared, leaving Gaius feeling like a total ass.

"He isn't a threat," Nessa said. "I think you scared him."

Gaius grunted. "I'll make it up to him by putting his ass to work. That boy has too much energy for his own good."

She gave him a weak smile, her eyes far too troubled for a woman who'd just come twice in a row. "I'd better not leave him alone up there for long or he'll dig a hole to Earth."

Gaius blinked at her, then finally got the hint that she was waiting for him to leave. He started for the door, then stopped, turning abruptly and catching her by the arms before she ran into him.

"Ness, please come to the house tonight. Moonrise just isn't right without you."

She looked taken aback by his emphatic tone. Her mouth fell open and her eyes widened as she struggled to find words. "I—I'll try. That's all I can offer, all right?"

With a sigh, he nodded. "Then I guess I'll take it. Have fun in the dirt, baby."

He gave her a peck on the cheek and opened the door, following her out.

She didn't come that night, nor the next or any after, despite Gaius' repeated invitations. What she *did* do was send him breakfasts and lunches daily with the same subtle suggestions that had him running down to the kitchen the very second he thought the coast was clear. He had her naked and moaning so many times he lost count, and Levi pretty much avoided popping his head in after getting it bitten off a few more times, which was more than fine with Gaius.

In the evenings, he would return after a few hours working on his own house to find her somewhere in the new kitchen, admiring the latest additions as it grew closer to completion. If he couldn't have her in his bed, he resolved to have her on every bare surface of this kitchen he was building for her, and in the one he'd be taking away when it was done.

Something had to give, but he was never good with words. He relied on his instincts in the arena, and his opponents had always been easy to read. Even out of the arena, he had no trouble reading any of the cues Ig or Bry or Levi gave off. They'd all taken to leaving the room as subtly as possible whenever Nessa came in, shooting him both hopeful and warning looks in equal measure. She meant a lot to them, it was clear. But she meant more to him. If only he could figure out what to say to get through to her ...

His heart got in the way, though, and all that ever came out was another invitation he knew she'd avoid. The words he couldn't speak wound up channeled into his house—by the end of the second month, the interior was mostly completed. Doors and windows had been installed, floors finished, furniture either built or delivered. He'd installed a lighting system similar to the one in her kitchen at Ig's house that adjusted to the time of day and would shift on command.

The only thing he hadn't finished was the kitchen. All that existed in that section of the house was an unfinished floor with vague, faded chalk lines where he'd marked its boundaries. Goddammit, he needed her to just come *look* to tell him how to finish it, because all he saw when he looked at the empty space was the old kitchen he'd made love to her in countless times over the past several weeks.

He glanced out the window and cursed. It was well past moon rise already, meaning he'd lost track of time, thanks to having actual lights in his house now.

His need for Nessa surged to the surface, a sudden craving for her sweet, curvy body beneath his own. She may have gone back to her cottage by now, but there was no way he'd get through the night without a taste of her.

CHAPTER
EIGHTEEN
NESSA

Nessa wandered through the new kitchen, admiring all the shiny surfaces. The equipment was installed, and she'd already begun moving supplies into the new pantry and the adjacent cooler.

She paused at the kitchen island with both hands resting against the cool, steel surface. Her body warmed and her mind filled with images of Gaius from the night before, making love to her against the island as she bent over with her bare breasts pressed against the cold, smooth metal. It had been yet another of many trysts they'd engaged in for weeks. The frequency was such that they'd almost become routine, except for the fact that her body ached for him whenever he wasn't around.

Every day, he'd arrive in the downstairs kitchen like clockwork after breakfast. Sometimes he'd simply bend her over the counter, lift her skirt, and ram into her while she encouraged him with eager moans. Other times he was slower about it and let her take control, so she'd push him to the floor or onto a chair and climb on, riding his cock like she couldn't get enough of him.

Then after supper was done and she'd finished prepping for the next day, she'd always wander up to the new kitchen, where Gaius would find her again. He'd arrive fresh and clean, yet still smelling faintly of sawdust or varnish or some other building material, and they'd make love somewhere in the new kitchen.

The new kitchen island was only the latest location. He'd turned her around for their second round, hoisting her up and climbing fully onto the broad, flat surface and making slow, deliberate love to her. He lay beside her afterward, half-naked as though this was a bed and the kitchen their bedroom. She supposed it was the closest they'd get to sharing a bed again, and she would take it. He rarely said much, but always invited her to come home with him, something she still couldn't bring herself to do, knowing their affair had an expiration date.

Nessa slid her hand along the smooth edge of the steel counter, already nostalgic for the previous evening. She supposed it was finally time for her to let him take out the dumbwaiter. She would mention it to him when he came.

If he came.

He was usually here by now, half-naked and buried inside her. She waited another half-hour before a sinking feeling settled in her belly. The suns had set and the moon was rising. He wasn't coming. For the first time in two months, he wasn't coming.

She left the kitchen with a sick feeling. It was bound to happen eventually. This wonderful affair they'd had all summer couldn't last, and she knew as much, but hated it anyway. She should have prepared herself for it better, but she'd wanted him so much she couldn't say no when he came to her every morning and evening. His absence now was all the more telling for how consistent he'd been for the last several weeks.

It was over.

Nessa sank down onto her sofa in the cottage and reached for her communicator. Even though her mother was rarely the voice of reason and would have nothing helpful to say by way of advice, she still found comfort talking to her. Her mother was the closest she could get to her father outside of his old kitchen, but the old kitchen was now filled with memories of all the trysts she'd had with Gaius, which meant it was the last place she'd find comfort.

"Mom, hi," she said when her mother picked up.

"Nessa, honey, I was just about to call you! This is so exciting. I have amazing news!"

Nessa sighed as some of her tension eased. Her mother was a wellspring of juicy gossip about the Hill Clan nobility. This was just the distraction she needed.

"I'm all ears," she said.

"All three of the clan leaders' sons are in the market! Rumor has it that they've all contacted Celestial Soul Mates recently. I told you it would happen, sweetie, and it has! It finally has!"

Nessa frowned, worried by the direction the conversation was going.

"Well, good for them. I'm sure the matchmaker will find them all wonderful mates."

"Oh, honey, you don't understand. Liora Delphine just called me! I literally ended the call right when you rang. She didn't want me to say anything yet, but I have to tell you. She has found you a mate, sweetie. It has to be one of them! I don't know which one, though... She only told me he was shifter nobility, but there's no way it could be anyone else. The timing is too perfect."

Nessa blinked at the floor for a second, not sure if she'd heard correctly.

"Ness, honey, are you there?"

"Y-Yeah, Mama, I'm here. That can't be right."

"Would I lie to you? This means you need to come home right away. I'm already planning a party to celebrate! Ms. Delphine will be bringing the guest of honor and you can meet him then. Isn't this exciting?"

Nessa struggled to bury the surge of panic and confusion of emotions bubbling up. "Of course it is," she said, hoping she sounded convincing.

"You don't sound happy, honey. Don't you want this? You know matchmaker Oracles are miracle-workers. One of them matched your father and me, and your uncle Alton with your aunt Julia. Now it's your turn."

"I am happy," Nessa said, straining through the tightness in her throat just to get the lie out. She *should* be happy, because if a matchmaker Oracle had finally found *her* a mate, that meant it shouldn't be long before they found the right woman for Gaius too. The woman who would finally inspire him to finish his house and be happy himself. That was all she wanted . . . for Gaius to be happy.

She let out a long sigh and repeated, "I am happy, Mama, I mean it. I just don't know if I can get away yet . . ."

"Nonsense. I know Ignazio will let you leave for this. In fact, I think I'm going to call and invite him to the party. All your friends should come. This is a wonderful event!"

Nessa's mouth fell open as she started to protest, but her mother kept going on about the party without a pause for breath. It didn't matter anyway; Ig and Bry were close enough to their extended circle of friends that they'd find out one way or the other, and her mother was right—they'd want to be there.

Finally, she assured her mother that she would plan to be there the next evening and hung up. She flopped down onto the sofa, her chest aching with a sense of loss for something that had never really been hers to begin with. How could she even explain to Gaius what had happened? Would he understand?

No, the fact that he hadn't shown tonight was enough of a sign that this was right. As much as she hated the idea of leaving, now was the time to go. She would leave a note for Gaius in the morning with his breakfast, which she would prepare early before leaving for home.

She roused and bathed, then slipped into her nightgown, but was too agitated to climb into bed. She needed something to channel this pent-up energy, and her thoughts went to the crate of Astreian Dewpetal flowers still sitting outside her door in their pots. They were the final touch to her garden and would give her the outlet she needed.

Not even bothering to change out of her nightgown, she headed for the door. But the tightness in her chest wouldn't ease, and by the time she reached for her doorknob, her eyes had blurred with tears and her throat burned with rising emotion.

The sudden knock on her door shocked her and she froze, blinking the tears from her eyes and sniffling slightly. "Who is it?"

"Baby, I'm sorry I'm late. Can I come in?"

"Gaius?" Nessa opened the door, her heart pounding, and he was there, dressed in clean jeans and a t-shirt, his hair still damp from the waterfall bath he'd taken. He looked way too good for her sanity. "I—I thought you weren't coming."

"Wild stallions couldn't keep me away from you, Ness. You gonna let me in?"

She hesitated, glancing over her shoulder at the little cottage's interior. So many nights over the past month she had considered inviting him to her bed to spend the night, but ultimately avoided it. Sleeping in the same bed together again would be *too* real, too much like they were a couple when she knew they could never be.

"Baby, it isn't a hard question," Gaius said, bracing his hand on the doorframe and leaning in. His scent overwhelmed her as his beard brushed her cheek and his lips found the sensitive spot beneath her ear. One big hand gripped her hip and squeezed. "I can't sleep at night if I don't have a taste of you first."

Oh god, she couldn't think with him that close. His sweet, woody scent made her forget all her boundaries, and the brush of his lips against her throat had her entire body awash with thrumming desire.

"You need me as much as I need you, don't you, Ness?" he murmured, crowding closer and looking down into her eyes. He hooked a damp strand of her hair over her ear and cupped her face, studying her for a moment with a look of wonder before he closed the distance and covered her mouth with his.

He hadn't given her a chance to answer his question, for which she was grateful. Yes, she needed him, but what good would it do to admit it?

Against her better judgment, she let him guide her backward and shut the door behind him. She could have one more night. Just one.

The next thing she knew, Gaius had lifted her in his

arms and carried her to the bed. He released her mouth and drifted his lips down the center of her chest, inhaling deeply as though her scent gave him sustenance.

Nessa combed her fingers through his damp, dark curls, enjoying the way the light caught the shimmering silver strands that were most prominent at his temples. He tugged the straps of her nightgown down her arms, freeing her breasts and cupping them in both his calloused palms. With singular focus, he lavished her breasts with attention, licking and sucking until she'd entirely forgotten why she'd ever had a reason not to let him into her bed.

He left her panting and writhing with need when he pulled the gown down over her hips and tugged it off with her soaked panties. Then he spread her thighs and wordlessly bent to cover her core with his mouth. He let out a hungry growl against her wet folds as he delved in, and Nessa clutched at his head, overcome by pleasure the second he began to tongue her clit.

Gaius' expert licks took her to the edge swiftly, the orgasm rocketing through her and persisting for several seconds, sustained by the slow, gentle licks he gave her as she came down from the high.

She stared up at him when he sat back on his haunches, still kneeling between her legs, fully clothed. Her orgasm had done nothing to shake the earlier uncertainty, and that uncertainty sapped the strength to tell him what she wanted . . . that she needed him inside her now.

But Gaius began to strip anyway, his blue gaze never leaving her face as he pulled his t-shirt off over his head, shifted backwards off the bed and kicked off his boots, then shoved out of his pants.

She closed her eyes for a second, too overwhelmed by the sheer, massive beauty of him. He had a Champion's body, with scars and tattoos that enhanced the hard planes and bulging muscles.

The bed shifted at her feet when he climbed back on, his warm skin brushing against her legs as he made his way back toward her. He pressed his lips to her left knee and slid both hands down her inner thighs, pausing to caress her still soaked pussy and tease until she arched her back with a moan.

Then he was over her, poised on both arms. The head of his stiff cock found her entrance easily and he shoved home in one smooth stroke, burying his face against her neck with a harsh groan of pleasure.

"Yes," she whispered, slipping her thighs up his sides and hooking her ankles around his waist. "God, yes."

It felt too good to have him completely naked and in her bed. They hadn't been completely naked together since that first weekend, and she hadn't realized how much she'd missed it. But naked meant vulnerable, and the second her next orgasm faded and his spasming cock eased inside her, that sense of impending doom rose in her once more.

Gaius slipped out of her and fell to the side, curling his big body around hers and holding her tight. His breathing grew even and slow, but Nessa still lay awake for some time, her cheeks wet with tears over what had never been hers.

CHAPTER
NINETEEN
GAIUS

Gaius woke to an empty bed and rolled over, stretching in the early morning sun and inhaling deeply, enjoying the invigorating scent of the Astreian Dewpetal flowers that had been lined up in pots outside Nessa's windows.

"Ness? Baby, where are you?" he called, but there was no answer. He got up and threw on his jeans, then followed the sounds of digging out the front door to her cottage. He blinked blearily at the figure digging in the flowerbeds outside the door.

"Levi... have you seen Ness?"

Levi set the multicolored fronds into the hole he'd dug and covered its roots with dirt.

"Nope. Just found a note in the kitchen this morning asking that I finish this up for her. Said she hoped to see me at some party her mom's throwing in a week. She didn't say anything to you?"

Gaius scrubbed his hand over his face and scratched his beard, frowning down at the other man.

"No," he growled and stalked back into Nessa's cottage

to grab the rest of his clothes. Where the fuck had she gone, and why hadn't she told him? He'd known something was up with her last night. Something in the way she'd clung to him and hadn't bossed him around the way she usually did . . . it had been all wrong. But he had hoped if he made love to her more tenderly, just to *show* her how much she meant to him, it would be enough.

Goddamn him, why hadn't he just asked?

He sat down on the bed to pull on his boots and something crinkled in the sheets. He glanced down to see a piece of paper sticking out from under his thigh with her handwriting on it.

Gaius, I am going home to meet my mate. As it turns out, I am not a lost cause after all, which hopefully means that you aren't either, because if the matchmaker Oracle could find my sorry ass a mate, there is definitely hope for you.

I will always cherish our time together. Be happy with whoever it is the the Oracle finds for you. I hope you find someone who brings you the inspiration you need to finish that wonderful house. It deserves a woman who loves it as much as you do.

Love always,

Nessa

Gaius surged up with a ferocious growl, crumpling the note in his hand as he stomped out the door. Levi jumped aside in a flash, clearing the way for Gaius as he charged to his transporter and headed back to his house. The meddling Oracle was going to hear exactly what he thought.

CHAPTER
TWENTY
LIORA

Liora settled into the transporter and keyed in her Astreia destination just as her communicator buzzed in her pocket. Events were converging as she had predicted they would. A little more than two months had passed since Nina Baxter's call, the one flooding Liora with concerns about Nessa's chosen path and Nina's uncertainty about whether it was good for her to be so far from the sons of the Hill Clans leaders when they were so close to needing mates.

The truth was that the three heirs to the Hill Clans leadership were indeed close to calling Celestial Soul Mates, but hadn't yet. She had different plans for them, and she was more certain than ever that Nessa's true mate was Gaius Osborn. She had finally called Nina Baxter the day before, giving her the good news that she'd found Nessa a mate who would satisfy the older woman's desires, but she refused to divulge his name. She preferred to meet with Nessa and Gaius individually to give them the good news first, though she finally acquiesced to Mrs. Baxter's insistence that she plan a celebration and that Liora should come and bring the lucky man.

The call she was about to answer was from none other than Gaius himself, who she was headed to now to give the good news to in person.

"Liora Delphine, Oracle," she answered as she watched the beautiful landscape of the shifter home planet speed by.

"Ms. Delphine. Gaius Osborn here. You've made one hell of a big mistake, lady."

Liora blinked out the window in surprise. "I'm not sure what you mean."

"Nessa's mine, and I mean to keep her. I don't want any other mate but her, so you'd best call her back and tell her you were wrong. Whoever it is you've got her running off to is the wrong man. She belongs with me."

Liora remained quiet for a moment, her lips pressed together as she tried to navigate this shift in events. It had to be Nessa's mother who'd somehow caused the misunderstanding. She shouldn't have talked to the woman before her daughter, but Nina had been her original client, so she felt a certain professional obligation to reach out to her first. She thought she'd have time to let Nessa and Gaius know before Nina could say anything.

Apparently, she'd been wrong.

"Gaius, you are a reasonable man. I promise there is an explanation. I'm in your area today. Why don't I stop by your house and we can talk about it?"

He was silent for a second before his deep voice came over the line again. "Yeah, sure, my address is . . ."

"Don't worry, I know how to get there. See you soon!"

She ended the call and settled back, letting the transporter navigate itself the rest of the way to her destination. She would fix this if it was the last thing she did.

When the transporter finally stopped, she got out, marveling at the change from the photos Gaius had shared with her when he'd first contacted her two years ago. Back then there had been little more than a bare foundation with a hammock strung between two big trees and a darkened fire pit. Now the entire clearing was occupied by a beautiful cabin situated in the perfect spot to capture both sunrise and sunset, the nearby waterfall adding to the idyllic atmosphere.

Liora walked up the front steps and lifted a metal knocker cast in the shape of the Blackpaw's emblem. It was good to see he hadn't let go of those old symbols. Gaius was definitely a man with a sentimental streak.

His big frame filled the entire doorway when he opened it and he towered over her, yet despite their difference in size and the fierce scowl on his face, he was as deferential as any of the men she worked with, bowing his head and ushering her inside.

"You want something to drink? I have fresh juice or tea. Made some herbed biscuits this morning. They're not as good as Nessa's, but you're welcome to them."

"That sounds lovely. Juice and biscuits." She smiled to herself at the mention of Nessa's name.

He returned to the living room and set a cup and plate down in front of her. Liora took a sip of juice and nibbled on the biscuit, humming in appreciation at its delicate crispness. He was a good cook, but she knew Nessa was better—it was in the girl's blood.

"Before you say anything, Gaius, I need you to know something about how I work. This isn't common knowledge, but it's often clear to me long before a client approaches me who they are meant to be with. Obviously I can't know this for certain without meeting a person, or at least knowing something about them in advance. But with public figures like yourself, it doesn't take much to draw conclusions."

His dark brows drew together. "Ms. Delphine, I already know who I want, you don't need to find me a mate anymore."

She held up her hand. "Let me finish."

Gaius pressed his lips together and crossed his arms, nodding for her to go ahead.

"You Champions are a unique group of shifters, the way you forego mating until after your careers are over. That habit makes my job both easier and more difficult. I have had time to watch your careers and prepare on the off-chance any of you reach out to the Oracles for help. For example, I'm already on the lookout for mates for your friends, Ignazio and Bryer, because I have a feeling they will be in the market sooner than they think."

Gaius let out a snort. "That'll be the day."

Liora waited patiently for a beat, then continued. "You have been more challenging, which is why it's taken me so long. I believe your temperament requires a certain . . . tenacity in a partner. The young woman I hoped to send to you is perfect, but her circumstances needed some finessing to get her on the correct path."

"Ms. Delphine . . ." Gaius started, but she continued despite the objections he spouted next.

"Her mother came to me when the girl was only a child. Despite her mother's wishes, I knew this young woman also needed a mate with as strong a will as she possessed. That's why I encouraged her mother to allow her to come work for Ignazio Karsten. Because I knew you would be here."

Gaius' mouth fell open mid-sentence and he sat staring

at her, dumbfounded for several seconds. "Nessa... You're talking about Nessa, aren't you? Are you saying I'm the mate she's supposed to be with?"

Liora nodded, wishing she'd been clearer with Nina when they had talked.

"Yes. I have known Nessa since she was a child. I always knew she'd need a particularly dominant male for a mate, and I didn't see that quality present to a desirable degree in the young men her mother had in mind. Trust me, I prefer to give my clients what they ask for, but when it's a parent asking for the child, I still need to keep in mind what is right for the child.

"Your retirement was fortuitous. I could see the pair of you on a path toward each other; Nessa's mother just needed some encouragement to let her go. Despite Nessa's headstrong nature, she cares greatly what her parents think. She always has."

"Then why the fuck does she think she's mating someone who isn't me?" Gaius snapped, waving the note in Liora's face. "She *left*. If she knew the truth, she'd have stayed."

Liora took a deep breath and leveled a stare at Gaius. "Did you tell her how you feel?"

"I..." He deflated. "Not exactly, no. I showed her... I built her this house. All but the kitchen, anyway."

"Has she seen it?"

His brows furrowed as he stared around at the house. Then he let out a long sigh. "No. She wouldn't come back, for some reason. I kept asking her to... and now she's gone off to mate some other..."

"Let me stop you right there, Gaius," Liora said, holding up her hand. "There is no other mate for Nessa. There never was and never will be. All she's doing is answering her mother's call to come meet a man who neither of them know the true identity of. Her mother is throwing a party at the end of the week in that man's honor. In *your* honor. I came here to tell you as much, and to bring you to that party. I had hoped that I'd be bringing the news to both you and Nessa, but it seems Nina Baxter has managed to screw up that plan. I asked her to wait so I could talk to Nessa first. My intention wasn't to cause confusion, but I realize my mistake now, and I'm sorry for that."

Gaius got up and started pacing the room, raking both hands through his mop of dark hair. He paused in front of the high, east-facing windows and stared at the empty space where a kitchen should be.

"How long until this party?" he asked.

"It's a week from today."

"You planning to hang around here until then?"

"I planned to visit a few friends while I was here, but I can adjust my schedule. Did you need my help with something?"

"Only need a woman's eye for a bit so I can finish Nessa's kitchen. I want this done before I bring my girl home."

Liora stood and walked over to stand at Gaius' side, rolling up her sleeves. "Just tell me what you need me to do."

CHAPTER
TWENTY-ONE
NESSA

Being back in her parents' house was bittersweet for Nessa. So much of her father still infused the place, but it was also clear her mother had done her best to move on. Thankfully, the kitchen was still the same, and Nessa could sit and commune with her father's memory here without the imprint of her mornings with Gaius that now tainted the old kitchen at Ig's house. She had told Ignazio to go ahead with the demolition of the old kitchen, though the new one would be difficult enough to work in as it was.

That was a complication she wasn't sure she'd be able to easily resolve. Not knowing who her mate was, she had no idea how to prepare for the possibility that he might not be okay with her continuing to work for Ignazio Karsten. But she had made Ignazio a promise that she would stay at least long enough to train a replacement, if it came to that. Her future mate would just have to deal with it.

It was so strange to think of her future mate in such abstract terms, but it was easier than knowing his true identity. Knowing who he was would make it too real, too inevitable, and she wasn't quite ready to let go of the memories of Gaius. She would have to soon, though. Her mother's enthusiasm kept her going, and she started to look forward to the party, at the very least as an excuse to visit with old friends she hadn't seen in a long time.

Halfway through the week, a rumor that was circulating made its way to her mother, and then to Nessa. She and her mother were finalizing the menu to give to the caterers her mother had insisted on hiring. "You are *not* cooking for your own party, Nessa," her mother had said. Partway through the debate about how much wine to order, her mother had dropped the bomb.

"Oh, did you hear that the Blackpaw found a mate? He was always your father's favorite Champion. I never agreed with his choice to give up clan leadership in favor of fighting. He'd have been mated a long time ago, if he had chosen his birthright."

Nessa's heart stopped and she had to bite her lip to keep from crying. "I thought Daddy was the one who disagreed with his choice."

Her mother tilted her head back and forth. "Oh, well, your father was always more liberal that way. You know how much he preferred sports over politics."

"I hope he's happy with her, whoever she is," she murmured, and she meant it. Gaius deserved happiness.

But her mother was already going on about other recent gossip, how the Hot Wings duo were neck and neck on their annual bet, and how the female champions were abandoning the superstition of waiting to mate until they retired.

"It's ridiculous for them to wait, anyway," her mother said. "The Blackpaw is so old by now, he probably isn't even fertile anymore. How is his new mate going to take the news if she can't have cubs because he waited too long?"

With that, Nessa couldn't sit still. She mumbled something about not feeling well and ran out of the room.

The one small blessing of being back in her home town was that there were no reminders of Gaius to taunt her. She could breathe a little easier out in the open, with the hot, dry air of the southern hills blowing across her skin. She wandered the quaint streets of the little village she'd called home until just recently.

It didn't feel like home to her anymore, though. Neither did her parents' house, despite the level of comfort she found through spending time with her mother again. She mourned her father less, at least. Her time in his old kitchen at Ig's had allowed her to finally come to terms with his passing and find a kind of compromise with her feelings there. She had his knowledge—all the things he taught her about cooking were things she would never lose. The old kitchen would be gone by the time she went back to Ig's, and while it left her feeling depressed, she preferred that sadness to the twisting pain in her heart over letting go of Gaius.

She needed a way to distract herself until the party, so she wandered into a dress shop to indulge in some shopping and personal pampering for the next couple days, and resolved to shove Gaius to the back of her mind. Something told her he would be happy no matter what . . . that there was no way he couldn't be with that house, even unfinished, and she highly doubted there was anything wrong with the man's virility. Good lord, that was the most farfetched thing her mother had ever suggested, but then Nina Baxter had never actually met the Blackpaw in person.

CHAPTER
TWENTY-TWO
NESSA

They had booked a huge outdoor pavilion in the nearby park, and guests were already arriving and milling about when Nessa arrived. The party planner who greeted guests with her mother had been a rare extravagance, but not a surprising one. This was the life Nessa's mother had always hoped for, but had appealed less to Nessa. She loved parties, but hated being the center of attention—being a chef allowed her to experience the energy and excitement from behind the scenes, and she was more gratified by how her dishes were received than she was by actually interacting with the guests.

She tried to pretend that today wasn't about her, but as she approached the pavilion along a path lined with strings of twinkling lights, heads turned and murmurs of acknowledgment picked up. She almost wished she'd chosen a less flashy dress than the deep blue body-hugging number she wore. It had reminded her of the color of Gaius' eyes, which was a dumb reason to buy it, but she hadn't been able to help herself.

Nessa's entire body flushed under the attention. She

wondered if her mate was here yet, and if he knew her identity or if he'd been kept in the dark the way she had. All her mother had told her was that he was shifter nobility and that the matchmaker Oracle was bringing him to the party.

Unlike her mother, she preferred not to jump to the conclusion that the man in question was one of the local clan heirs. Once she'd pried the exact quote from her mother, she'd insisted that it could mean anything. There were hundreds of bear shifter clans scattered around Astreia. The northern ones were more numerous than the southern ones. It could just as easily be one of the heirs to *those* clans as it was one of their own.

As she greeted the friends and acquaintances, she kept her eye out for an unfamiliar face. Would she feel a spark? Would she ever get over this feeling that she was betraying Gaius by even being here?

Everyone kept congratulating her and asking who the lucky man was, to which she could only reply, "You'll see." She didn't want to admit that even *she* didn't know who he was, which was honestly starting to get old.

After about an hour, she went to her mother, irritated by the conspicuous absence of anyone who could even remotely be the guy she was waiting for. "If he doesn't show soon, I'm leaving, Mom."

"Just a little longer, honey!" her mother said. "Ms. Delphine just called. She's bringing him now. Your friends Ignazio and Bryer are on their way too."

"She didn't happen to tell you his name, did she?"

Her mother's gaze darted around the room and she pressed her lips into a hard line. "No, but it has to be one of the three clan leaders' sons, otherwise I've just insulted all three clans by not inviting them."

"You could have fooled me, because they're here . . ."

Nessa nodded toward the main entrance to the pavilion where a large group had just arrived. Her heartbeat sped up at the sight of the three handsome shifters and their entourages spilling into the big space and spreading out. The party itself picked up considerably with their arrival.

Nessa refilled her drink, hoping more alcohol would help calm her agitation. She forced herself to continue mingling, though all she wanted to do was stand and watch the entryway for signs of the matchmaker Oracle, who she only vaguely remembered from meeting her as a child.

"Excuse me," a smooth, deep voice said, and Nessa turned suddenly, nearly spilling her wine. The big, brown-haired man who stood behind her smiled and reached out a hand to steady her. "Whoa, didn't mean to scare you. You must be Nessa Baxter."

"Yes, and you are?" she asked, flinching at how snappy her response came out.

He only smiled more broadly. His beautiful, straight white teeth and keen brown eyes fit perfectly in his strong, tanned features. "I'm Jacob Hansgen. Heir to the Green Hill clan. My friends and I have a question to ask, since you seem to be the guest of honor."

Two other men strolled over with fresh drinks, one of them handing Jacob a full glass. They introduced themselves as Gunther and Teague, the heirs to the Rock Hill and Sunset Hill clans.

"We heard you're friends with a matchmaker Oracle," Gunther said.

Nessa blinked at the trio and then said, "So it isn't either of you three?"

"What isn't?" Jacob asked.

"My mate. Neither of you three are my mate. If you were, she'd have arrived with you, or so I hear."

Teague laughed. "God, I wish. No, your mate is on his way with the Oracle. We know that much, but . . . are you saying you don't know who he is yet?"

Nessa's spine straightened at the appraising look he and the other two were giving her. They liked what they saw, which bolstered her confidence.

"I have no idea, so whoever it is, he'd better be worth the damn wait."

The trio shared a look and Jacob cleared his throat. "If I tell you the truth, will you put in a good word with the Oracle for us?"

"A good word? I thought you three had already met with a matchmaker Oracle."

"Not yet . . . We plan to as soon as we can. Rumors started flying the very second it came out that we were even thinking about it, and all of a sudden, everyone believed we'd already done it. Of course, we're aware of how that might look to Celestial Soul Mates . . . which is not good. So, we were hoping since you're friends with one that you could help set the record straight. We *want* to meet with them, desperately, but we want to make sure they know the three of us are a package deal."

"Oh?" Nessa asked, intrigued as she took in all three big, handsome men. The darker-haired Teague shot an almost desperate look at Jacob.

"We're a bit attached to each other," Jacob said. "We want to share a mate."

"Oh," Nessa said, giving them all a sly grin. "That sounds lovely. And I'm a little sad that I'm not the lucky girl who gets to be the center of your attention."

Jacob laughed and shook his head. "You won't be sad once you find out who your mate is . . ."

Nessa stood up straighter, more than ready for the news

when more commotion came from the entrance to the pavilion.

Gunther leaned in and whispered into Jacob's ear. Jacob turned and nodded, then stooped down to whisper to Nessa. "I guess I won't need to tell you, after all. You can see for yourself."

CHAPTER
TWENTY-THREE
GAIUS

Ignazio and Bryer led the way up the path to the pavilion while Liora and Levi walked on either side of Gaius. His adrenaline spiked the way it always had just before beginning an arena match, and his bear was roaring in anticipation of the spectacle.

When they reached the arched entrance, excited murmurs picked up from inside and the crowd parted to make way. Ig and Bry mostly blocked his view, and he was sure the excitement was directed toward the pair of them, which was perfectly fine with him. Gaius appreciated the diversion, preferring to maintain the surprise for as long as possible. He just hoped the dramatic entrance would be a grand enough gesture to make up for his lack of honesty with Nessa.

He should have told her he wanted her the very second he knew without a doubt she was his. Her desire for him had been so plain he thought she would come around, but had no idea how much stock she'd placed in the matchmaker Oracle's choice.

There would be no more confusion or doubt after

tonight, and he resolved never to let those three words go unsaid again. He loved her. He'd probably loved her from the day they met. He had certainly known she owned his heart after their first night together.

The excited chatter picked up in volume as eyes fell on him and the crowd parted further. Past Ig and Bry's big frames, he caught a glimpse of Nessa's warm, light-brown skin and black hair tucked up into a complicated coil before she was obscured by a trio of bigger bodies stepping forward. He growled. This was taking too damn long.

Levi bumped him with an elbow. "Chill out, man, she's right there. Those three are the bears who are in on the surprise. They just asked to be introduced to their hero in exchange."

Ig and Bry stopped and stepped to the side, making way for three bear shifters to approach.

Gaius had to restrain himself from roaring for everyone to just get out of his way. The first of the three paused and hesitated when Gaius stared him down. "You're in my way."

"Okay . . ." the big brown-haired bear drawled. "Guess you really *are* her mate, aren't you? Lucky girl." He gave Gaius a once-over, then winked and stepped aside. The other two looked equally pleased with themselves when they parted, finally revealing a very irate Nessa.

She couldn't have looked more beautiful, her generous curves all wrapped up in a vivid blue dress. The shimmering mod-cloth fabric cradled her luscious breasts perfectly with gathered lengths stretched and tied at the back of her neck. He ached to hold her again, to sink inside her and hear her calling his name.

The irritated look on her face faded and her big brown eyes widened in surprise when she saw him. "Gaius? What are you doing here?" She darted a glance past him toward the way he had come. Then her jaw dropped and her cheeks flushed. She let out a soft "oh, my" that was muffled by her hand flying to her mouth.

"I'm here for you, baby. Ms. Delphine, tell her who you found for her." He kept his eyes fixed on Nessa's, which were now starting to brim with tears.

He barely heard the matchmaker Oracle's announcement over Nessa's squeal of pleasure. She was in his arms so fast the rest of the world disappeared.

"It's you. Oh my god, it's you!" Nessa repeated over and over, both laughing and crying as she peppered his face with kisses.

Gaius held her in a death grip, inhaling her sweet, nutmeg scent like he'd been starved for air. "You're damn right it's me, Ness. It's always been me, you crazy girl."

Around them, the entire pavilion was filled with hushed murmurs as the news made its way to the outer reaches. Whispers of surprise that the woman in his arms was the Blackpaw's mate only made him hold her tighter.

He'd caught wind the past week of the rumors flying around about his having found a mate. Somehow even retired Champions couldn't hide from paparazzi. After griping about it to Liora, she assured him she hadn't told a soul, but anyone who found out she was visiting him in person would likely draw conclusions.

But none of that mattered now, not when Nessa was finally in his arms again. He gently set her down, then dropped to one knee, wincing at the spike of pain that shot through both joints.

"Oh, Gaius, your knees!" Nessa said, urging him to stand.

"Baby, I need to beg your forgiveness, and there's only

one way to do that. The first night I saw you in the moonlight at my house, I knew I had to have you, not because of anything the matchmaker said, but because from that moment on, everything about my life felt complete."

A hush fell over the crowd as he spoke, and his bear rumbled in satisfaction the way it always had when he was in the last stages of a match just before certain victory. Nessa's cheeks were wet with tears and she bit her bottom lip as he continued.

"Baby, I'm sorry I never told you that I knew. It shouldn't have taken an Oracle coming to prove it to you. I should have said so. There are so many things I should have said, but the most important thing is this: I love you, Ness. Will you *finally* come home with me tonight?"

Nessa nodded and laughed. "Of course, Gaius. There is no place on Astreia I would rather be. Take me home."

As he hoisted her in his arms and kissed her, the crowd's cheering rose around them louder than his bear's roar of triumph. He would have happily carried her straight out to the transport and left right then, but she wiggled and protested, so he reluctantly set her down again. He found himself standing face-to-face with Liora Delphine, and another older woman whose lovely features gave away her identity as Nessa's mother. But she didn't look nearly as thrilled about the situation as her daughter did.

"Gaius," Nessa breathed. "I'd like you to meet my mom, Nina Baxter. Mom, I guess you were wrong, after all."

"Pleased to meet you, ma'am," Gaius said, dipping his head politely. The woman kept scowling. It might have been her daughter's smug tone, but Gaius would bet it was all his fault somehow.

Nessa's mother gave him a scathing look, then turned to glare at Liora. "Is *this* what you call shifter nobility? This man forfeited leadership of his clan. He has no legacy to offer my grandchildren!"

Gaius bristled and Nessa blurted out a protest, but Liora held up her hand and leveled a cold stare at the other woman.

"Mrs. Baxter . . . Nina . . . You came to me in good faith more than twenty years ago to secure a mate for your daughter when she came of age. As unprecedented as that is, I always had a high regard for your husband and his family, so I agreed. However, what *you* desire is of little consequence to the task you set for me. Your daughter's mate is more than worthy, and while he may not hold rank in his clan any longer, he is likely the most highly revered bear shifter of mating age in all of Astreia. More than that, your daughter loves him." She nodded toward Gaius and Nessa.

Nessa's mother turned back to them, jaw clenched. She looked Gaius in his eyes for a long moment. "You had better make my daughter happy. And I want grandkids sooner rather than later, *if* you think you're up for it." She shot a glance at his groin and twisted her mouth derisively.

"Mother!" Nessa snapped. "For your information, there is no man on the planet who could make me as happy has Gaius does. I've wanted him for months, but because of your stupid contract with the matchmaker, I believed he wasn't meant to be mine. But he *is* now, and you had better believe I'm keeping him, babies or no babies!"

Her mother deflated when she looked at Nessa and finally gave them a grudging smile, much to Gaius' surprise. "Oh, honey, are you sure about this? I wanted more for you."

Nessa sighed and shook her head. "No, you wanted more for *you*, but your life isn't over. Maybe you should, I don't know, meet with a matchmaker Oracle for yourself. I know a pretty amazing one." She grinned at Liora Delphine, who smiled in return.

"Come, Nina," Liora said gently, taking Nessa's mother by the arm. "Your daughter's right. She has always known what she wants, despite you trying to orchestrate a relationship for her to your own tastes. Let's divert that energy to find a mate *you* would be happy with. I think I know just the man, and he happens to be in attendance tonight."

She gave Gaius and Nessa a conspiratorial wink before leading Nina away.

Gaius looked down at Nessa. "Baby, I hope that's the last person who stands in our way, because I mean to take you out of here now. Anyone who tries to stop me does so at their peril, and they *all* know how much power I can bring."

She stared up at him through wet lashes. "Trust me, I can pack a punch too. Let's go."

They were accosted from all sides with well-wishes and congratulations, but true to her word, Nessa didn't falter. By the time they made the door, she was running ahead and laughing with his hand gripped tightly in hers as he tried to keep up. His knees ached, but he didn't care a bit, not when his girl was finally going home with him.

CHAPTER
TWENTY-FOUR
NESSA

Nessa itched to wrap herself around Gaius, to strip him and make love to him in celebration of this wonderful revelation. But she wanted to get home even more and needed to let him drive. *Home* to the skeleton of a cabin that she had already mentally finished over and over in her mind. She didn't even care if it took months before they had walls and windows. It would always be home now. The Astreia night flew by, the transporter flying over the landscape as quickly as it could go, but it wasn't a short trip back to the northern mountains.

"There's our moon, baby," Gaius said, pointing out the domed glass roof. He squeezed her hand and she squeezed back, leaning her head against the glass and staring up at the silvery moonlight.

"I missed you so much," she said with a sigh.

"Me too, Ness," he said, raising her hand to his lips to kiss the tops of her knuckles.

"Sorry about my mom. She has a habit of blowing things out of proportion. If I'd just waited one day . . ."

"Not your fault, baby. I should've told you how I felt when I knew."

Nessa's chest ached as she recalled all the times he'd asked her to come home with him. She knew he wasn't big on sharing, but that last night they'd been together had felt different, and not just because she knew she was leaving. Gaius had been different—more intent on her pleasure at every step. Not that he didn't always care about her pleasure, but there had been a desperation in both their caresses.

She cleared her throat and rasped, "When did you know?"

The silence stretched for several beats before he lifted her hand again and pressed his lips to her palm this time. His beard was luxuriant against her skin, and she kept her hand against his cheek when he released her, running her fingertips over the silky fur.

"From the first day," he said, his voice catching on the last syllable.

Nessa didn't respond, too shocked by the confession to know what to say. She remembered the day they met and how he'd gotten under her skin almost instantly and had stayed there. Had her bear's agitation been attraction—a certain understanding that she'd met her mate? Yet she'd passed it off as irritation at his bull-headedness.

"Oh, Gaius, I'm sorry I'm so stubborn."

His deep chuckle reached her a second later. "No, you're not. But neither am I. We were made for each other, Ness. No sense fighting who we are."

She smiled and fell into a reverie as she stared up at the moon. It always seemed to remain in the same place no matter how far they traveled, a persistent, undeniable presence. She would never doubt her heart again.

HEART OF THE BEAR CHAMPION

Nessa woke with a start, heart pounding. She stared up at warm wood beams above, barely registering what she saw over the flash of images from the dream she'd been having.

She'd been at the party waiting and waiting, but no one had come for her. Everyone else in the crowd had gradually paired off, the handsome sons of the clan leaders getting their wish and finding a statuesque woman who looked nothing like Nessa. Even Bryer and Ignazio had headed off with someone, a single blonde woman whose face she couldn't see, but who she knew without a doubt belonged with the pair.

Yet still she remained standing alone in the middle of the crowd, forgotten.

The Oracle had finally arrived and given her the bad news—that she was unmateable. Nessa had nodded as though unsurprised while secretly shattering inside. She still couldn't shake the feeling of loss and rolled over, pressing her face into the pillow.

Gradually, the dream faded, and she looked up again at the gleaming wooden beams, then to one side where a set of glass doors overlooked a wide balcony, and beyond, where morning mist still hung heavy over the trees. She knew that balcony...

She turned her head, her heart racing again as she sat up and looked the other direction. Morning sun streamed in through cathedral windows, turning the railing of the interior landing to fiery gold and washing across the crisp white comforter that covered her.

She gripped the smooth, fluffy cover in her fists, then spread her hands out, pressing it flat. A comforter that was on a bed, in a room... a room that hadn't been more than an empty platform open to the elements the last time she'd seen it.

Now, as she peered around, she remembered with vivid detail the evening she'd seen this space, but the difference in it now was shocking. There had been nothing but bare studs and sawdust before, but now the floors were highly polished wood inlaid in lovely starburst patterns, and there was furniture: a wardrobe, a dresser, and bedside tables, all of which looked expertly crafted by hand.

And a bed. A bed with massive carved-wood posts that were reminiscent of the front porch posts of Gaius' house, only with floral carvings covering the surface. Lengths of gauzy white fabric draped between them, swaying in a faint breeze that flowed up from the first level.

How could this be? She'd fallen asleep the night before on the ride home, imagining all the ways she would help Gaius finish the house. Somehow everything she'd pictured had come true, but more spectacularly than she had even thought.

She pushed the covers off and slipped over the edge of the bed. Her reflection in a full-length mirror caught her eye first, and her heart warmed at the sight of the red threadbare flannel draped over her body. Gaius' shirt. He'd carried her to bed asleep and put her into his shirt.

She wished like hell she'd been awake for that. For all of it.

Heavy footsteps echoed through the house, making their way up the stairs in a deep rhythm. Gaius appeared, buck naked and tousle-haired with two steaming mugs in his hands. Nessa watched him in the reflection as he paused and took her in, his gaze raking over her in a look of such blatant possessiveness her core warmed.

He took a few more steps and set the mugs down on the

nightstand, then moved behind her. Nessa licked her lips at the sight of his arousal thickening between his thighs the closer he got to her, until it was obscured when he paused just behind her.

"Welcome home, Ness," he said, slipping close and sliding his arms around her waist. He rested his chin on top of her head and she leaned back into him, letting out a soft hum of interest when his hardness pressed into her lower back.

"You should've woken me up last night," she murmured.

"I should've carried you home with me a week ago, whether you liked it or not," he replied, grazing his lips over her temple and jaw. She tilted her head to the side to give him access to her neck, shivering when he kissed the sensitive spot beneath her ear. He slipped his hands up her sides and over her breasts, tugging at the buttons of the shirt until they came free and the sides fell open, revealing her to him in the mirror.

His heated blue gaze met hers in the mirror as he cupped her breasts, hefting them both and tweaking her nipples until she gasped. Slick heat flooded between her thighs, her core throbbing with need for more.

Gaius continued to brush soft kisses over her neck and shoulder as he tormented her breasts, alternating between harsh plucks and pinches and soft caresses of her nipples.

Nessa craned her neck, desperate for his mouth on hers. Gaius complied, hungrily clasping his lips over hers as he spun her in his arms. He crouched and cupped her under her bottom, hoisting her in his arms as they kissed. Eagerly, she wrapped both arms and legs around him, relishing the long-missed sensation of his skin against hers, the glorious furred muscles of his chest hard beneath her breasts.

Gaius carried her to the bed and climbed on, never once relinquishing her mouth even for a breath. When he found the center, he settled on his haunches with her still wrapped around him, her core pressing hotly against the base of his cock.

She tilted her hips, aching for more contact, and moaned at the sliding friction he granted when he moved his own hips in kind. His cock dragged along her soaked channel and she braced her hands on his shoulders to lift up and give him access. All it took next was for her to succumb to gravity and he was inside her, and they rocked against one another.

They moved slowly at first, still kissing, but then his tempo increased and Nessa's crescendoed to match as her pleasure and need grew in equal measure. She tore her mouth away from his and tilted her head back with a gasp of ecstasy, meeting each driving thrust with a desperate twist of her hips seeking to pull his thick length as deep into her as possible.

Somehow this time was even more frenzied and desperate than the last. It was as though they'd spent a lifetime apart and not just one week. They'd left too much unsaid and undone the last time. This time she was all-in, and she needed to make sure he knew.

"Gaius, please!" she begged, surging up and clinging to him, burying her face in his neck as she sought to get even closer. He thrust harder and faster, digging his fingers hard into her hips as he guided her rhythm to match his own.

"You're mine, Ness," he growled into her ear. "Never leave me again."

"Never," she agreed, her entire body set alight when he brushed his lips over her shoulder and opened his mouth, grazing his teeth across her skin.

Nessa pressed her face tighter against his neck and opened her mouth in turn. If she was his, then he was hers, and she meant to prove it.

Gaius let out a groan when she summoned her bear's spirit and manifested the sharp incisors she needed to mark him. At the same time, he pressed his pointed teeth against her own tender skin.

They sped up their fucking, frantic now with the promise of permanence. God, she wanted this so much more than she had ever wanted anything else.

With his teeth pressed into her skin, her pleasure soared and her body rocketed to an explosive peak unlike any she'd experienced. Reflexively, she bit down, and the coppery taste of blood flooded her tongue.

Gaius roared, his cock surging violently into her. Pain shot through her shoulder, but it only served to heighten her rapture as his seed filled her core.

They clung to each other tightly, breath rasping in tandem as their bodies continued to tremor with the aftershocks.

Nessa pulled back and kissed the side of his face, then his mouth, ignoring the glistening swipe of red that colored his lower lip. They had done it. They were one now—irrevocably, permanently mated, and she couldn't be happier.

He groaned into the kiss, his tongue sweeping deep and sliding against hers. His cock surged and swelled inside her again, but she pushed back, looking up into his lust-drenched gaze.

"I love you always, Gaius. *Always*."

His desire retreated slightly, replaced by a smile of adoration. "I've loved you every second since we met, Ness, and I will love you for all the others too."

He started to tilt them down to the bed, but Nessa

yelped in alarm. "Wait! You're all bloody. Don't mess up the sheets already! Here..."

She clambered back onto her knees as she hurriedly slipped out of the ratty old shirt and pressed it to his shoulder. Gaius gave her a long-suffering look.

"What? Everything is so perfect. I don't want to mess it up."

"But you'll ruin my favorite shirt?"

"Psh, it's got more than enough character to handle a little bloodstain. Besides, what better memento to carry it than this shirt?" She pulled it away from his shoulder and stared, tilting her head in wonder at the perfectly sealed wounds that were now no more than a series of upraised scars in his skin. "How...?"

"Champion training, baby," he said, pulling the shirt out of her hand and pressing it to her shoulder. "Talk to your bear for a second. Hold her close to the surface, just enough that she's almost coming out, but don't let her. That power will heal you quicker than you would by keeping her buried. You should listen to your bear more often."

Nessa closed her eyes and did as he asked, but her bear was already right there waiting, so it didn't take much effort.

"Attagirl," he said, then pressed a quick kiss to her shoulder. He handed the shirt back to her and she shook it out, but couldn't even make out the blood against the multicolored check of the fabric. Lifting a hand, she ran fingertips over her shoulder, smiling up at Gaius when she felt the four upraised bumps where his teeth had pierced her skin and the wounds had healed over.

"Now you're stuck with me," she said.

Gaius snorted. "Does that mean you're back to cooking

my meals? Because I've been mighty spoiled the last few months, then you left me high and dry. My knees missed you."

"Just your knees?" she asked, giving his freshly hardened cock a tickle.

He abruptly grabbed her behind the knees and toppled her back against the pillows. Nessa squealed and laughed as he settled between her thighs, peppering her face and shoulders and chest with slow kisses.

"My knees, my belly . . ." He lifted his hips and eased into her slick depths again. "My cock . . ." As he pumped into her, he lifted up, bracing himself on his elbows and staring down into her eyes. "My heart."

"Oh, baby, my heart missed you too," Nessa said, then pulled him into a kiss. She pushed her hips up into him, meeting him thrust for thrust until they were both gasping and shaking from another shared climax.

Gaius fell to the side and hooked an arm around her, pulling her tight against him. When they caught their breath, he rumbled against her ear, "So about that cooking..."

CHAPTER
TWENTY-FIVE
NESSA

"Be careful, or I might start to think all I am to you is a cook." Nessa punched Gaius' shoulder lightly and rolled over to get up, eager to explore what other new changes he'd made to the house since she'd first seen the almost bare frame two months earlier.

"You're everything to me, Ness. I should've figured that out ages ago and said it a hundred times. I mean to make up for it every day for the rest of our lives."

Looking back over her shoulder, she found herself overwhelmed with love and utter adoration at the sight of his handsome, rumpled visage. His hair stood on end in all directions, the silver strands glinting in the early morning sunlight. Impulsively, she reached over and tousled his tangled curls. She leaned in to kiss him, then turned and hopped off the bed.

She shrugged back into his old shirt and padded across the room to a door to one side of the fireplace that hadn't existed last time she was here. Inside she found a large and mostly empty closet, a quarter of it filled with soft flannel shirts and jeans and work boots. It smelled of sweet evergreen wood and was illuminated by a skylight.

To her right just inside the closet was another door. She opened it and peeked in, letting out a sharp gasp at the sight of the vast, luxurious bathroom complete with a giant sunken tub large enough to fit two and a rain shower built from the gold-hued stones the waterfall coaxed out of the mountain in its path down the peak. She took a leisurely stroll through, marveling at the attention to detail. Like the bedroom, it was even more beautiful than she could have pictured on her own.

Nessa came to stand in front of the mirror over the counter and stared at herself for a moment. Like the closet, sunlight filtered in from a series of skylights high above and lit up her flushed cheeks. Gaius filled the second doorway behind her that led back out into the bedroom on the opposite side of the fireplace from the closet.

"Gaius, this is beautiful. Somehow I don't feel the least bit worthy." She smoothed her hand over the shining surface of the counter, similarly crafted from a large slab of the same golden stone as the shower and polished to a high shine.

"It isn't what you pictured? We can change it."

"God no! Don't change a thing. It's perfect . . . *better* than I imagined."

He grinned at her in the mirror. "Wait'll you see downstairs."

Nessa took his proffered hand and let him lead her down the stairs, which were now fully finished with shining wood banisters. She stared out the massive two-story windows as they descended, breathless at the sight of the spectacular Astreia sunrise. Both big orange orbs were chasing each other up past the horizon, casting twin sets of rays down over the trees in the distance. The river fed from the waterfall shimmered as it passed by the deck outside.

This was Nessa's home now. This view, this house, and this man. She paused at the bottom of the steps, still drinking in the vista, and turned back to express her love to Gaius again when something oddly familiar and out of place caught her eye.

She turned her head and her heart stopped.

"Oh Gaius . . ." She was only able to get the two words out before her eyes teared up and her throat constricted. Her hand flew to her mouth as she collapsed against his side, unable to hold herself up from shock at the wonderfully unexpected sight before her.

Gaius hooked his arm around her waist, supporting her, and kissed the top of her head. "It would've been a shame to see the whole lot go to reclamation after all the times I made love to you in that kitchen."

She swiped at her eyes, but was unable to stop the flow of tears and the soft sob that welled up. It was too much. Not only had this wonderful man finished his house just the way she had imagined . . . better than she had imagined . . . he had also installed a kitchen that there was no mistaking was for *her* and her alone.

It wasn't a new kitchen, by any means. The old enameled equipment with its copper accents had been polished so the copper gleamed. The worn wood-slab island still had the same well-seasoned surface. Even the deep copper sinks had been installed—also polished and shining in the sunrise. Her father's entire kitchen had been transported to this house. Every last piece. And she had no idea how in the world she would ever thank Gaius for something so grand.

He shifted his stance beside her and rumbled uncertainly. "Ness . . . You do like it, don't you?"

Shakily, she inhaled and spun around, surging up into his arms and claiming his mouth in a kiss, at a loss for any words to express exactly how she felt.

But Gaius needed no words to grasp what she needed from him. He carried her into the kitchen and set her on the island in the center, then proceeded to make love to her, re-christening every surface as if the room were brand new. While they made love, Nessa reveled in the absolute fullness of her heart, and knew without a doubt that she had earned this love and would never, ever let it go.

EPILOGUE
GAIUS

One Year Later

Gaius swept his brush in one final coat over the windowsill and stood back to admire his work. A pleasant nutmeg scent wafted from behind, and he unconsciously reached back, pulled Nessa under his arm, and bent to press a kiss to her forehead.

"It's done," she said. "You've outdone yourself again."

He grunted, knowing full well that the nursery was only the beginning of the renovations he'd have to make to the house over the next two decades. He set the brush back in the empty bucket at his feet and pressed his palm over Nessa's round, pregnant belly.

"Don't get too attached. They'll have it torn to pieces the second they can crawl."

Nessa groaned. "Of course it had to be twin boys. Me, stuck in these mountains with the testosterone brothers. After dealing with Ig and Bry and you and Levi, I deserve a daughter, dammit! It's all I asked."

"Soon as they're out of you, I'm happy to work on putting a girl in you, baby," he said with a cocky grin.

"We'll work on that when the time comes, I promise. This summer, my mission is to find Ig and Bry a mate."

"One mate? Singular?" Gaius asked, lifting an eyebrow and looking down at Nessa. She grew pensive, her brows scrunching together and he knew she was thinking about Bryer, who was still in the League hospital recovering from a near-fatal arena injury.

She swallowed and nodded. "I had a long talk with Dr. Taji. She believes finding him a mate is the only way to get him fully healed. But I don't see those two lasting if one of them gets mated and the other doesn't, and their godforsaken *bet* isn't doing them any favors, so . . ."

Gaius heard the equivocation in her voice and chuckled. "What'd you do, Ness?"

"Oh, I just called Liora Delphine and told her to be on the lookout. Bonus points if she can find a substitute chef for them while I'm on maternity leave. After the babies are born, I'll need the help anyway, especially with the feeding regimen Dr. Taji recommends for Bryer after he's released. It's going to be a long, hard road for him. I want . . ." She paused and bit her lip, her eyes searching his.

Gaius knew what she was thinking. Ever since their mating, he'd been a new man. It hadn't even required a special diet, though Nessa's cooking didn't hurt. His knees never once twinged, and some of the gray had even left his hair. It was almost as if his bear had been reborn twenty years younger.

He'd even entertained the idea of competing again, but dismissed it the very second he learned of Nessa's pregnancy. He had more than he needed right here with her and his construction business, so he was more than certain Bryer's doctor was right. The boy needed a mate.

"You want them to be happy."

"Yeah. If you and I could find each other, there has to be someone out there for them. Hell, Liora even managed to find my mom someone. Mom's on Cloud Nine, now that the elder Jake Hansgen's professed his love to her. She finally got the clan leader she wanted." She shook her head, smiling inwardly, no doubt remembering the ordeal Nina Baxter had put them through the prior summer.

"Well, if anyone can find those boys a mate, that Oracle can. But I suggest you not discount the power of bribery. Last time she visited, I caught her snooping through your cookbooks. She seems to be attached to that cake of yours."

Nessa's brown eyes twinkled when she looked up at him. "My recipes were the way to your heart, after all. They're bound to work on a matchmaker's heart too."

ALSO BY OPHELIA BELL

You can find a complete list of Ophelia's books by visiting opheliabell.com.